(S)KIN

ALSO BY IBI ZOBOI

American Street

Pride

Black Enough (Edited by Ibi Zoboi)

Nigeria Jones

WITH YUSEF SALAAM

Punching the Air

(S)KIN

IBI ZOBOI

An Imprint of HarperCollins Publishers

Versify is an imprint of HarperCollins Publishers.

(S)Kin
Copyright © 2025 by Ibi Zoboi
All rights reserved. Manufactured in Harrisonburg, VA,
United States of America.
No part of this book may be used or reproduced in any manner
whatsoever without written permission except in the case of brief quotations
embodied in critical articles and reviews. For information address
HarperCollins Children's Books, a division of HarperCollins Publishers,
195 Broadway, New York, NY 10007.
www.epicreads.com

Library of Congress Control Number: 2023947876
ISBN 978-0-06-288887-7

Typography by Jenna Stempel-Lobell
24 25 26 27 28 LBC 5 4 3 2 1
First Edition

For all girls who are not afraid
to kiss the sun

Daughter. Come here. Grab a pillow and set it on the floor.
Pass me the comb and pomade. Sit down. Scoot back.
Come closer. Are you tender-headed? Your hair has grown.
It is like your bones—tough and made of memory.

Each strand is an ancestor, you know. Each ancestor
has a story, you see. Bring them all together like so,
smooth down with oil, wrap around your fingers,
cross over and under, twist, curl, be tender,
and you will know the truth of what we are.

These braids are to remind you of all the mothers
who came before you, like me, your dear mummy.
This ritual is so that we sing the song of our skins
over and over again like a hymn.

Your people want to shout their stories up to the sun.
They want you to never, ever forget them, so you
do not forget yourself, darling,
and how girls like you
were born out of
flames.

Your hair is done now, petit fille.
Turn around. Smile for your old mother.
Look how pretty you are! Get up.
Is the mortar ready? The moon is high.

Who hurt you, chéri? Go after them.
Make sure they deserve it.
We are not evil, you know. Just complicated—
like this world. No good, no bad.
Just consequences—

You have a name? You have a face? You have a place?
Good. Go get them! I know it hurts.
Nothing painless about war. Nothing sweet
about vengeance. Just duty. You owe it to us.

You owe it to your foremothers.

They call us old hag, but you are young hag.
They call us soucouyant, but we are just sipping
from the chalice of life. They call us lougarou,
but we are only shape-shifting like the waning
and waxing moon. Be careful now.
Never let anyone see you.

I will look away. Hush, baby! You have to get
used to it. Just breathe and breathe and
before you know it, the entire night sky
will be yours. You are so pretty up there, too.
We are stars, baby. Stars!

Do what you have to do to survive
up there and—   down here.

And pray that no one finds your skin
in the mortar, an heirloom and our protector.
Pray that no one knows our story.

Remember, there are others. But we keep
to ourselves. Better divided than united.
Always remember that home is wherever
you are in the world and in the cosmos.

There you go! They better watch out!
Wait!
Come back before dawn.
The morning sun will be the death of us.

All the stars, comets, and meteors are kin—
the souls of women and girls
who were never able to return to their skins.

Don't forget. Return to your own skin—
your own magic, your own power.
Do you hear me? You say, "Yes, Mummy chérie."

Now go! And do not be late for school.

ONE

MOTHER MOON

——MARISOL

Nightmare

Mummy prays over me as if I am the worst evil.

Our bathroom is small, but she's managed to pull
in a nightstand covered with candles and incense
as I sit in the tub hugging my knees and
hiding my tears.

It's like that old movie, *The Exorcist*,
but instead of a priest, my own mother
is talking the fire out—
is purging the demon out of my body.

Today was one of the coldest days ever,
but tonight,
I   will   burn.

Steam and smoke fill our little apartment
in Flatbush, even as all of New York
is covered in icy snow.

Mummy clutches her Bible against her chest,
closes her eyes, throws her head back, and recites
an old prayer. Not Creole or patois
because I don't understand a word.

We were born there and
we are making a new life here—
if we can call it living.

This corner of Brooklyn could be
anywhere in the Caribbean
with all its island flavors and sounds.
The smell of curry stew and jerk chicken
grilling outside a restaurant
and the lingering scent of
Haitian pumpkin soup
from New Year's Day wafts
into our apartment.
Soca and compas rhythms
blasting out of car speakers
make our walls   shake.
My dancing partner is often a lamp or
the swaying curtains from an
opened window—
except the cold reminds me that we are
now on the other side of the sun,
where our magic may not be as powerful;
as healing; as deadly.
Even though there are more of us here,
we hide.

Mummy makes me feel sinful with her cacophony

of chants, Bible verses, and hallelujahs.
Her American dream for repentance
and devotion won't work on us here.
We

          are

               nightmares.

II

I wince because the tingling has started.
Then the heat, the sweat, the throbbing pain, then
Mummy's escalating voice. I clench my fists
even though soon, I will no longer have human hands.
I squeeze my eyes shut even though soon, I will still see
everything from the sky. I take deep firebreaths
even though soon, my lungs will be made of flames.

Mummy raises one arm up to the ceiling calling down
      everything that is   holy
                    to help me become
      everything that is   unholy.

Our eyes meet and this is when we are no longer
mother and daughter.
We are comrades in arms ready to wage war
against the night; ready to fight for the true
version of our story.

There's a tiny window where the
night sky calls out to me.
One last time, she gives me a name.
"Jean-Pierre. He accused me of stealing,"
she whispers. "There was money missing
from the cash register and he threatened
to kick us out." Then she recites
the Lord's Prayer.

When I can't think normal thoughts
like my favorite song and
my favorite dances and
my dreams for the future;
when the memory of everything
that makes me human becomes
a dark cloud of rage;

when I hear the suctioning sound
of my body collapsing in on itself;
when my skin peels away
like an ebbing ocean wave;

when my cells ignite, bones dissipate,
and my brain, heart, lungs, nerves, and blood
become a plasma of hydrogen, helium,
neutrons, and cosmic dust;

when my insides ignite like the
BIG BANG
that created the universe,
and my soul becomes electric,
and shifts into a rod of lightning,
and then,
a shooting star caught on fire—

I am becoming
what my mother
is trying to conjure—

a monstrous thing that needs
God
even though
we are made of the
same   magic.

III

And I   shape-shift
into an otherworldly self.
I become
a mangled, collapsed version of myself
within a raging ball of fire
and
a deep hunger pulls me out of my skin,

out of that tub, past Mummy's prayers,
and out of the small bathroom window
and past everything that is trying to
extinguish all that I am.

Our new home with its
thick walls and locked doors
wants me to stay trapped in my skin—

but I am fury and flame.
I am a ravenous creature
born out of war and
all I want to do right now
is inhale life so that I
can keep   on   living.

It always feels like   It always feels
like wanting to vomit my insides—
nauseating, sick to my core,
pulsating pain,
      and
      instead of a scream rising
from the pit of my firesoul,
      I   combust—

and leave it all behind:
my skin, my human self,

and all the holy things
that come with being
a child of God,

as Mummy would say.

Who made me like this?
Hungry and full of rage,
but even as a ball of vengeance,
I know that my destruction in the sky
is small
small
like
a tiny white lie.

But someone is always praying for
my destruction—

Flight

The shoreline of our island
used to be our border—the place
where when we reach it, we know
we have to return to our skins
and   go home.

We arrived last month,
just before Christmas
and the bright, colorful
lights and decorations
appeared to be celebrating
our homecoming for
winter solstice—

except we are not the sun.

We are its daughters.
We are meteors and shooting stars
who have to learn to live as humans
when the old moon wanes and waxes
like a temperamental mother.

Here in Brooklyn,
brick, metal, concrete, and bright lights

take the place of mountains, palm trees,
and colorful bungalows in the distance.

We live above a yellow sign that says
Island Bakery.
A man named Jean-Pierre is the owner.
Mummy told him that I am good at baking.
It's a lie. It's only so that we live
somewhere that is susceptible to flames.
In a bakery, no one will suspect us
of starting a fire   like they do back home—

if it comes to that.

So we work in exchange for a one-room apartment.
I take over Mummy's job on weekends
while she cleans fancy homes alongside some
of the other immigrant women she has met here.

And on weekdays, I am supposed to go to school.
I started just last week
on the first Monday of the new year.
It's my first time going to school
on this side of the sun.

School in America was Mummy's promise to me.
School in America was Mummy's

Christmas present to me.

"There is a school down the street,"
she'd said. "We can register you because now
we have an address and a bank account
that tells them that we live here,
but we will need to show them papers
that tell them we *belong* here.
They have names for us, Marisol.

"Newcomers. Refugees. Migrants.
Undocumented.   Illegal.
But they will never call us

monsters."

Except Mummy doesn't know that
in my new school, I already feel like a
monster.
So I hide in the shadows of tall bookshelves
in the library, which are like the shady palm trees
back home—anchoring old stories to the real world;
anchoring me to my secret magic.

I've brought home some of the books.
They call them old stories,
fantasy and folklore.
I call those stories   my life.

But still,
Mummy brings me more books
(given to her by the families she works for).
I read everything, I listen to every whispered word,
I watch every movement, and I wait
for my turn to   kiss the sun.

She can't keep me trapped in here forever.

Is this the life she dreamed of for me?
Is this why we left the place where even in our
monstrosity, even in our magic,
                    our myth and folktales were
                    both food and shelter?

II

The skyscrapers here keep us from flying as high
as we can because people seem to want to live
in the clouds. They want to kiss the sun too.
But not with flaming wings.
Not with myth and stories
trapped in their bodies,
like me and Mummy.

They want the power without the magic.

I fly and fly and fly and—

my magic is old, and old magic
has to adjust to new places.
New skies, new stars, new nights.

III

Mummy always wanted something more
than life on the islands, more than a life
boxed within the lavish rooms of the
Hibiscus Resort. We didn't live there.
But we cleaned those rooms as if preparing
to rest our tired bodies on the bleached linen
and feather-filled pillows each night.

Resort work on an island is the only
life we have ever known. But Mummy
always dreamed of the horizon
where the sea meets the sun;
where the world stretches
much farther than our
mountains; much
wider than our
shoreline.

Mar y sol.
That's what she named me—
sea and sun—

as if my being born was to fulfill
this dream of hers; that I would one day be
a compass, a lighthouse of a girl guiding her
to my namesake.

Mummy says that I am also Maria de la Soledad,
Our Lady of Solitude.

If the sea and sun are her dream
for me, then the other meaning of
my name is a curse.   Forever alone,
forever my mother's only daughter,
forever a sole shooting star in the night sky.

We left a place where we make sense.

What good is a flying fireball witch
among all these city lights?
And from the sky, it feels as if I have
flown out of a cage, but I am no bird.

I will not be pecking at scraps
for sustenance. Food does not fuel
my firesoul,
not even bread.

So as a ball of flame, a flash of light,

I aim for the starless sky.
I aim for the spiritless souls,
      emptied of dreams, emptied of knowing
            that monsters rule the world.

GENEVIEVE—

Nightmare

I've had to learn to pray on my own.
Not because I wasn't raised religious
or whatever, but because there are things
that scare the shit out of me—

and I believe in magic, in monsters,
in things that go *bump* in the night.
I swear one of them will snatch me
up out my bed.   I blame my father

and his PhD in anthropology and all
those weird masks and knickknacks
and old-ass books around the house.

So tonight, I kneel and clasp my hands,
even as the new babies holler and wail,
and my skin feels like it's on fire.

"Please, God. Please, let me sleep tonight,"
I whisper.   There's a bottle of melatonin
gummies on my nightstand.   But I'm afraid
of anything that'll pull me deeper into
that dark place where nightmares are born.

No one in this house will sleep
with the new babies—   twins.
A girl and a boy. Bethany and Elliott.

But it's not just the new babies that keep me
up at night.   It's my fucking skin—

I borrowed my stepmother's gloves
so I don't hurt myself—
no matter how butter-soft Kate's leather
driving gloves are, I still manage to scratch
      the enflamed rashes until I bleed.
I don't dare take the gloves off when I try to sleep,
or else I'll peel my skin with just my short stubby nails.

It's that bad. The allergy. The eczema.
Whatever it is, it's worse at night. For a year now,
I've been feeling as if
      my skin will burn and melt
            right off my fucking bones.

The cold wind outside rattles my window.
That was the first thing to wake me.
Then the itching. Like a billion tiny needles
poking and prodding all over my body.

I try to distract myself the way Dad showed me—
What do you smell? Soothing lavender oil and the

memory of tender, soft baby's breath.
What do you feel? The pits of hell, I swear.

But I promise I've been good. I've been good.
What do you see? The new moon casting a shadow
of the tall elm tree onto my bedroom ceiling.
It sways against the light, and it looks like me
when I dance. Long-limbed and graceful.

Except I wish I was just a shadow of a girl—
no face, no hair, no skin—just a silhouette
of how beautiful I can be when I dance,
                    and only when I dance.

On some nights, the tree's shadow is the
only thing that lulls me to sleep—
I can almost hear its quiet lullaby in a language
I've never heard before—
a song from a faraway place and long-ago time.
One night, as my whole body felt as if it would
combust into flames, I cried out to the
dancing shadow tree and said,   "Mama."

II

I dream of her.   But those dreams are
not of a mother holding me close, shushing me,
and smoothing down my thick, curly hair—

those dreams are not of a mother
making some old, smelly remedy
that would   heal
my   skin—

when I dream about my mother,
there is always   fire.

"Daddy? Did she burn, like, in a house
        or something?"
I had asked my father one day when I was little.

"No, honey! Why on earth would you think that?"
He'd blushed and glared down at me with tired green eyes.
Then he nervously ran his fingers through his wispy brown hair.

Kate was weird, too, when I asked about my mother.
She went pale and pushed her blond hair behind her ears.
She was right there in the kitchen when I'd asked.
Then she turned away, hiding her face.
She holds the pain of my father's betrayal in her eyes.
And when she looks at me, she sees the proof.

My biological mother was a Black woman.
I was raised by my white father and his white wife.
I wear this betrayal on my skin and in my hair.

But that doesn't matter now, because

Kate got what she's always wanted—   babies.
Kate is my father's wife. She has always been my
father's wife.   And she's now a mother.
Just   not   my mother.

III

I try to think of love songs and of my boyfriend
Micah's wide, cool hand resting against the small
of my back. But the babies' crying
        is like dragging a fork across a plate.
They start squealing at the same time at
just past two in the morning.
        It's been three weeks now.

I sit up in bed and rub my arms and legs.
The silk pajamas slide against the thick layer
of ointments, gels, and oils I'd rubbed on last night.
One baby stops crying. I can hear Dad's footsteps
up and down the stairs and his scraggly voice
yes-honeying Kate left and right.

Then Kate yells something at my father. I perk up.
Dad doesn't say anything back. Kate has been mean
to everyone since the babies, since the pregnancy,
since the fertility treatments—
        and maybe, since I came into her life
        as a baby. Seventeen years ago was too

long for her to remember how it feels
to hold a newborn in her arms. But I was
not hers—   I belong to my father
and some ghost of a mother who I swear
        haunts me in my dreams.

Kate must've opened her bedroom door 'cause I hear
        her say, speaking clearer now,
"It's my decision to make, Daniel. One of the
cleaning ladies offered to help, so I hired her.
End of discussion!"

"I wish you'd run it by me first," my father says.
"An interview? A background check? A reference?
You can't just have anybody around our newborns, Kate!"

Their bedroom door slams shut. Kate's careful, tired
footsteps race down the stairs. A baby starts to cry.

I could cry, too, for my father right now—
he doesn't deserve this. Kate doesn't deserve him.
        And I'm in the middle.

I could put on my headphones and block out all of it.
But Dad will still be awake. He has to teach in the morning—
        take the train up to Columbia University.
And I have school. And the babies will be at it all night.

My mother tree is dancing and singing that lullaby and—

IV

It's morning. Finally—
the sun shines today and it's
unusually warm—hot, even—for January.
Everything is fuzzy with blurred edges,
like I need glasses or something, but—
my skin is soft, soft,
like whatever new steroid-infused
lotion my dermatologist prescribed
is working. Thank goodness!

My hair cooperates too.
The thick curls hang loose and
the ringlets frame my face just right.
No frizz, no dullness, no dryness and—

I can wear anything today.
Acrylic, polyester, nylon, spandex.
I have dance class too.
I'll choreograph a new piece—
contemporary with a nod to both
Dunham and Horton.
I can focus on technique and form
and not the burning pain—

I can let Micah caress my bare arms
without wincing, without hiding.

I can smile and take selfies and—

The day—muted and warped—
slips away before I even get dressed.
Night becomes a thick blanket slowly
easing over a sun that hasn't even
reached the sky yet—

I'm naked and the floor is hot. Hot.
I tiptoe trying to get onto a rug and—

The hardwood becomes a bed of
coals? Embers? A straight-up fire!
A scream from the pit of my belly
rises into the air like flames—

My room is not my room anymore
and a white-hot darkness swallows me
whole and—   The sky is wide
and cool but   I'm still burning.

              And flying—
          flying?
Balls of flame dart pass me like comets.
And—   I feel so free and wild

and hot.   Still hot, hot.
And hungry.   So   hungry.
But for the first time this reoccurring
nightmare becomes like   a dream

come true.   In my sleep I'm soaring
and hot.   Still hot, hot—
and hungry.   So   hungry.

And I fall and fall and fall and—

I jolt awake, sweating. Itching. Burning.
It's still night,   near dawn.
The babies are still crying.
Kate and Dad are still arguing.
My skin feels even worse and—
I'm back to this nightmare
               that is my reality.

Fire and brimstone—
that's the only way I can describe
the world I sink into when I sleep deep.
      Pure hell—

And I sob right along with my new brother
and sister   with no one to comfort me.

Flight

I wish I was made from silk—spun from
insect larvae that forms cocoons as they go
through metamorphosis; shedding and rebirthing
at each stage of their life cycle—

Egg (skin), larva (skin), cocoon (skin), moth (wings).

I'd rather be born out of a cocoon than
be born out of the womb of some unknown,
invisible mother. Silk makes sense to my skin.
    So does the moon—

I grab one of my expensive-ass silk robes
that's both soothing and cooling and wrap
myself within its soft, nurturing fibers,
    like a cocoon—

I have to wear organic everything, natural,
made from the earth and all things living—
Plants, insects,   people, maybe.

II

It's almost five in the morning and
in a couple of hours, the sun will rise over Brooklyn.

My sleepless nights are an unhealed wound
and yesterday will bleed into today.

Coffee keeps my eyes wide, my brain buzzing,
and I wish so bad that the caffeine would
peel back my skin too.   It hurts that bad.

Green or black tea is better, so is matcha.
I have to watch everything I eat, but I swear
it's not what I put into my belly that makes it worse.
I think it's what's happening outside my body,
like, up in the sky; the moon and stars or something—

It was Kate's idea to have a rooftop garden,
and it's the best thing she ever did for me.

On nights like this, it's where I escape to.
On nights like this, my skin is begging
for more than fresh air. It craves the universe.
And all I have to do is look up to see
that the moon is always full
                    on nights like this—

III

On the roof of our brownstone, everything is
covered in a thin layer of ice and I should have
on a coat. My phone is tucked into the pocket

of the robe, but everybody is asleep, especially Micah.

We were up video chatting until midnight when
he straight-up started snoring on me—
and I was left with crying babies, the darkness,
    the burning, and my own
    firebreaths.

On the roof is where I find myself
and hear my voice, and taste freedom—
I click on a few of the string lights and the outdoor
chairs are turned down against the table.

I don't sit. I stand there beneath the cold
gray sky with just a silk robe and I should
be freezing, but   this feels good.

Slowly, I untie the belt and push the robe
from off my shoulders—   The cool winter
wind kisses my bare skin and   it's almost
like Micah's lips but   I'm still burning.

I let the robe drop to the ground, the fake turf
beneath my feet feels like needles or hot coals
    like in my nightmares—

I'm fully naked now under the new moon
in the beginning of January, at the start

of a new year, in the heart of Brooklyn.
I lean my head back and stare up at the sky
to let everything, everything wrap me within
its frigid arms—   I want to fly!

IV

The moon is my very own spotlight and—

Something bright   darts across   the sky.

A flash of lightning?
    A shooting star?
        A comet?   Meteor?

I look for   another sign.
Something that lets me know that there is more
out there than just   burning gas that forms
constellations.   I'm too frozen
(not from the cold but from shock)
to move. I don't walk over to the telescope
Dad got me a few years ago when I
started being obsessed with the night sky.
Not in an astronomy-geek kind of way,
but in a I-belong-up-there-too kind of way,

and   I want to fly—

Every time I see the sky like this
I get so hungry   I could eat the world

and—   The door to the roof creaks open
and I jump.   It's too late to grab my robe
because Dad is standing there staring at me, squinting—

——MARISOL

Fever

The thing about monsters and spirits,
the thing about myths come to life,
and folklore that sprouts wings,
is that most people will
never stop to wonder
and look up
at the sky
to see

me.

II

Jean-Pierre lives where there is space
between the houses and his fancy cars are
crammed in the driveway like unused,
plastic-covered furniture.
With this American dream of his,
with this big-city living of his,
he has forgotten the stories
of scorned island girls and women:

We come for you   in the night.

He has never bothered to ask Mummy
how we left the islands—
by plane, by boat, by foot, by hoofs,
by fins, or by wings.

He has never asked us about the
mortar or suspected our hidden magic.

He counted his money instead,
accusing my mother of stealing—
even after forcing long hours
into our days; forcing a fake smile onto
our weary faces; forcing a life of servitude
onto our life of power and magic.

He never dared to find out if we are
what we really are.
Here, ambition takes the place of
superstition
and the immigrants like us
have turned their eyes away from
the wonders of the unseen world.

Maybe we are better for it.
They will not hunt us
if they don't believe   we exist.

III

I have learned to seep through
cracks in the wall. I have learned to
ease through crevices in the concrete.

Shape-shifters
        like me have to become the elements—
humans and beasts of the earth,
birds of prey and gusty wind in the air,
        rain showers and morning dew on flowers,
and little fires everywhere.

                I am made of vapor and vengeance.
                I am both ghost and deadly smoke.

Jean-Pierre rests peacefully next to his wife,
who is as sweet as the bread pudding she makes
for the bakery. She lets me and Mummy take
day-old loaves at the end of our workday,
        but she tolerates her husband's cruelty.
        She is trapped like us, so I leave her alone.

        Jean-Pierre's fat belly is even rounder
        as he sleeps; he is even louder as he snores
        without a care in the world in his big house,
with his many businesses and immigrant workers
who do not have papers and proof of our existence.

When I am smoke, I do not light up the room
with my muted flame. When I am vapor
I can still see, and smell, and taste, and
know, and   remember—

                but I must never, ever turn to
                look at my reflection in a mirror.
Never—

                There is a huge one on the other side
                of his bedroom wall, tempting me
to see what kind of
monster   I really am.

                But in this moment, I am more hungry
                than curious. I am more thirsty than vain.
                So as quick as a flicker of light,
                I descend on Jean-Pierre's chest—
                as smoke, as heat, as a gruesome force—
for vengeance,
for sustenance
and   I

inhale   deep, deep—

And he stops   snoring.

GENEVIEVE—

Fever

"Gen? Is that you?" my father asks, rocking a baby in his arms.
"For Christ's sake, Gen! Where are your clothes?"

I quickly grab my robe. *Shit. Shit. Shit.*
"I was hot," I whine, embarrassed.
"Dad, you brought the baby up here?" I ask,
distracting him from his own question.

"No, you first. Why are you here
in freezing temperatures with just a robe?"

"Come on, Dad. You know how my skin gets. It's worse.
It's like a sauna in my room. Kate got the heat up 'cause of the
babies and—   She'll be pissed if she knows you're
here with . . . which one is that again?"

"I don't even know at this point," Dad says, rocking the
baby in his arms so hard, I want to take it from him.
"We both needed some fresh air. And, Gen, put on a coat!"

"And, Dad," I say. "Bring that baby back inside!"

But my father looks as if the life has been drained out of him.
Dad and Kate are both supposed to be happy now that the twins
are here, but they're just, like,   over it—

The baby cries even louder and I wish I could tell them apart

and—   it's like a magnet pulling me closer and closer

and—   I want to hold it so bad, cradle it in my arms

and—   my father lets me take the baby

and—   he plops down in one of the chairs, holding his

        head in his hands.   He's so tired

and—   I'm so, so hungry

and—   the baby keeps crying

and—   crying

and—   it's so warm in my arms

and—   my silk robe is the only layer between its skin

and—   mine. I can't tell who it is, Bethany or Elliott—

        Blue for boy or pink for girl, but I don't believe

        in that gender binary bullshit

and—   I hold my baby sibling against my chest

and—   something hot washes over me

and—   fuels that ravenous, empty hunger

and—   I inhale deep, deep, deep—

and—   the baby stops crying.   Finally.

—MARISOL

Breath

We let them live. We are not that kind.

At the very most, Jean-Pierre will be
struck with a sudden fever; struck with a
sudden shortness of breath; or worse (better),
a sudden paralysis where he is close enough
to death so that I am close enough to life—

I'm full from someone else's life force—

The journey back to my skin is much
quicker. I am a flash of lightning
in the sky. I am a shooting star
aiming for home through an
opened apartment window—

When I land in the tub as a shimmer of light,
my skin comes to me like a moth to a flame.
I am air filling the balloon that is my body.

Everything still burns when
I am myself again. Mummy is always
there sitting in the dark with a
bucket of ice next to the tub—

She turns on the faucet of cold water
and quickly closes the window.

It all happens in reverse—
Mummy's now soothing voice, the throbbing pain,
the sweat, the heat, the tingling—
She rests both hands on my skin and prays
away everything that is
unholy
to help me become everything that is
holy—

Human.   Girl.   Normal.
With arms instead of flaming wings;
with dark brown skin instead of firelight;
with a hunger for bread and a thirst for water
to remind me that I am now earthbound—

Until the next month
when the new moon
cracks open our universe
to ignite our flames.

The dawn light slowly brightens the apartment
and I am reborn—

Me and Mummy's eyes meet, and this is when
we are once again mother and daughter.

We are comrades in arms ready to fight for
a peaceful reality; the freedom to exist
as the others do—without magic
but powerful just the same.

I take in the cool air in the apartment
because Jean-Pierre was always
stingy with the heat, and I am full again.
My breaths are steady and slow,
no longer like a dragon in the sky.

II

"You did good, Marisol. Very good, ma fille,"
Mummy says, making small circles on my bare back.

I did it for my mother—
My victims are her enemies. Mummy says
our enemies are the ones who
threaten our survival.

But if my mother has taken me from my home,
from everything that I love and loves me back,
then she has threatened my own survival.

And maybe, she   is my enemy.

III

After hunger, after we've sipped
from the souls of our victims,
there is an exhaustion so fierce
and a sadness so deep,
I can sleep for a week.

It is as if we've just eaten a meal
too big for our stomachs—

"Why do we have to keep doing this here?"
I ask my mother with a small, quiet voice.
"I thought that once we left the islands we
would not have to live like this."

"Ah, Marisol," my mother says.
"Our stories do not belong to the land,
they belong to our souls. Wherever we go,
our magic comes with us—"

But this magic, this power
only makes sense on the islands—
What good is it here if we are
still living like we are powerless?

She pours ice into the bathwater. It helps us
settle back into our skins. It is never cold enough

for me. We did not have to do this on the islands.
A mountainside river was always our healing balm.
My foremothers have only known rivers.

Here, we make up new rituals as we go along.
Here, rivers are murky graveyards for a city
that wants to drown the magic that lives in the
souls of its people.

IV

I sit back in the tub
easing into the ice water,
settling back into my skin,
and I remember home.

On the islands, we would sleep
for the whole day after shifting and flying.
Our sisters in magic would cover for us
at the resorts, at the marketplace,
in the homes of the wealthy people—
wherever we found work.

On the islands, we were a community of
lougarou, cow-footed girls called la diablesse,
seal-skinned and devil-horned jab jab, mermaids,
soucouyant, and every folktale come to life.

Our stories were never dead. We were always
walking (or flying) amongst the living—

The city noises outside keep me and Mummy
company. She hums a long-ago and faraway
island song as she prepares for a day at the bakery.

After the bath and after I am fully human again,
I sleep on a mattress pushed up against a wall.
Old sheets hang from the windows. Chipping white paint,
a single flickering light bulb, and deep melancholy are the
only decorations we have. Not even a stove or fridge add
warmth to the adjacent kitchen. Jean-Pierre said we have
to buy our own appliances. *With what money?* One pot,
two plates, a set of cutlery, and two small suitcases were
the only things to come with us from the islands—

And the heavy wooden mortar.
But that is not a possession,
more like a protector.

Mummy's protector.
It does not belong to me. Yet.

I stay in bed until it is time to go to school.
"Can you bring me some coconut bake?" I ask Mummy.
I eat out of boredom, not out of hunger.

"I will have to pay for it since Jean-Pierre
doesn't trust me," Mummy says.

She is wearing her uniform from the resort
back on the islands because what else are
we supposed to do with free clothes?
It's a white dress with tiny red hibiscus flowers.
No one here will know unless
they've vacationed there—

"Jean-Pierre will not be able to come in
for a long while, remember?"
I say, pulling the old blanket over
my shoulders. Guilt stirs in my belly like hunger,
but I've learned to ignore useless human emotions.
I am wearing a thin nightgown.
We have never updated our wardrobe for a life of
twenty-degree weather, cold winds, snow,
long noisy nights, and   loneliness.

Mummy turns to me with her hair pushed back into
a small afro puff, as always, and smiles bright.
"Ah, yes, thank you," she says. "Now we are free
to do as we please. Then I will bring you
coconut bake, salt fish, a slice of avocado,
and a cup of coffee with
sweetened condensed milk."

I don't tell her that I'm not that hungry.
She will be paying for it anyway, with
what little money we have.
Mummy wants to still be good—

But this small box of a home has never been enough
compensation for all the hours we work at the
bakery. They told us how expensive it is
to live in New York. But Mummy believes
that we can still survive on very little—

I do not want more food and bread.
I wish she had really stolen that money instead.

Life

As soon as the apartment door slams shut,
as soon as I hear Mummy's heavy footsteps
going down the stairs, I rush straight to the
window and press my face against the cold
glass to soak up the sun, the sounds, the people.

Three weeks here, and I am ready to claw at the walls.
Three weeks here, and if only I could just walk the streets
as just human, as just a girl to sip from this chaotic energy,
this frenzied existence called America.

People my age are laughing and living free.
Their bodies are wrapped in hooded blankets.
Hats and scarves shield their faces as if winter
is something that will eat them alive.

I wonder what their days are like
when they're not in school.
What do they do with all their time if they
have to hide from the cold? Mummy says they
watch TV and go on the internet until their
brains turn to porridge. I wonder if any one
of them knows that people who look like them
can shape-shift and fly. I wonder if they
can shape-shift and fly.

How many of us are out there
making a new life out of old magic?
I want this new life too.

I want the freedom of living in a world
where no one will accuse me of being a
monster—
I want to live in a place where reality
is the only existence I know, and science
is the only thing that can make sense out of
the senseless, and everyone sees me as only
human.

So I dig into my suitcase
for a pair of jeans and a sweatshirt
that says *I Love New York*—
a gift from a tourist at the resort.
The lock and chain on the door is supposed
to keep us safe. Mummy has a key, but no one
will want to steal what we own, so I open it,
step out, and close it behind me, unlocked.
I will walk the streets as if I have
two feet and not wings.
On the night of the new moon, I will hunt
for Mummy.
On the other days, I will live free
for me—

The scent of baked bread reaches me before
the cold does. The stairs and door
leading to the streets are next to the bakery.
I will be long gone by the time Mummy notices.
I would have already tasted this American dream
and be full of freedom.

But just as I open the building's door,
my mother is standing there.
"Where do you think you are going?" she asks.
"It's too soon to return to school.
You have to rest   and hide."

In no time, we are back in the apartment
with a tray of breakfast food
and this time, Mummy makes me lock the door,
not to keep anyone out, but to keep me   in.

"You cannot roam the streets here, Mari,"
my mother says. "Everybody belongs to a
piece of paper. Every soul is marked with a
number. With no ID and no passport,
if something happens to you, they will
bury you in an unmarked grave
as if you never existed."

My mother exaggerates.
It's either we hide or we die.

It's either we leave the islands or we die.
It's either we live the same life or we die.
But how is this the dream?

So I pull out an old, tattered book about
a dark girl like me who wants blue eyes
and step into the pages of a world
full of people whose lives
are as lonely as mine.

Except where is this girl's power?
I keep reading, hoping that her magic
is in the blue eyes that she wants—

And from the closed window,
I listen to the voices on the street.
I watch the people come and go,
their warm bodies slicing through
the cold air. And I will   not wait.

II

Tonight, it is Mummy's turn to shift and fly.
The new moon calls us on any one of the
three days between its waning and waxing—
like our firesouls gaining momentum
and energy each time we sip from a life force.

Never have me and Mummy shifted and flown
on the same night, under the same new moon.

So without praying away evil
and conjuring holiness,
without God and His forgiveness,
without dreams of a better life
in a crowded city and in a starless sky—
I prepare Mummy's mortar by rubbing
coconut oil into the space where
her skin will be stored—

And tonight,

she   will   burn.

III

The mortar is a giant, heavy, cylinder-shaped bowl
that narrows at the bottom. The pestle that goes with it is
long gone now, lost to the past generations of mothers it
belonged to. Their figures are carved at the bottom, and
balls of flames in different sizes are painted around the top.
It tells the stories of what we are and how we came to be,
like cave drawings, like hieroglyphs documenting our truth:

We exist and we are real.

Mummy says the mortar was passed down to
her from her mother, and her mother's mother
like DNA, except we are made of fireblood.

It holds the ghostly remnants of the shed and
withered skins of my grandmothers, and I have always
wondered why it cannot come with us in the sky—

like the ogresses and witches with their flying mortars
and brooms in the stories from around the world.
This mortar cannot float on water, neither.
It cannot be a boat or a plane.
But it is a lifeline.

It is like part of our body, Mummy's body.
And she will have to die in order for it
to belong to me—

"Soon, Mari, this will be all yours.
This is the curse we must carry.
This is our punishment,"
Mummy always says.
"But two skins cannot occupy the same pot."

So instead she makes me use the tub
until the night when her fire dims and
it will be my turn for my soul to burn bright

and fly higher than the moon so that I can
kiss the sun.

IV

But if the sun rises
without us returning to our
vulnerable skin left alone
while we fly at night,
our skin will burn and sizzle like
salt poured onto a fresh wound.

And with no skin to return to, we would make a
meteor or a comet out of our ended lives;
we would be a star holding a
permanent space in the universe like
an ancestor forever bound
to a celestial existence.

That is what happens to us. We do not die,
we get absorbed into the cosmos—

Some call it heaven, but it would be
our hell—

V

I pass the mortar pushed up beneath an opened window.
Her skin is in there, shrunken into a floppy mass of
flesh. I stare at it as it pulses and glows with life,
waiting for its owner to return like a pet left alone.
I stare up at the polluted sky. Too many lights here.
Too much noise here.
And I don't think. I don't consider the consequences.
Because I am hungry
for something more than souls.

I want to live free.

So I close the window.
My heart pounds.
My breaths quicken.
Fear is a useless human emotion.

The curtains drop limp and
wrap me within their cool arms.

Then I rush to the bathroom
and close the window there.
The chill in the air lingers as
I watch the night sky through the cloudy glass.
She will need to get back in.
Mummy will need to get back into her skin
so she does not stay as a fireball forever.

I swallow back tears because   because
she is still   my mother.

                                        But—

        I refuse to live this new life in this new country
in my mother's shadow. I will claim this apartment
as my home. I will get furniture and paint the walls
colors to remind me of the islands—
        peach, turquoise, lemon yellow, mango orange.
I will have friends over.   New friends.
The ones I see outside.   And maybe,
I will go to a university.
I will throw out everything that belongs to Mummy
and create   my own real world—

But   I forgot
that my mother is
made of vapor and vengeance   too;
both ghost and deadly smoke   too.

VI

My mother's firelight brightens the whole apartment
as she approaches the window. It rattles, like hurricane
winds threatening to take down the whole building.
                "Stay out, Mummy," I whisper.
                "I cannot fly high if you are
                the only one lighting my flame."

Mummy is a raging hot wind now.
When we first arrived here, I'd gotten close
enough to see her morph into a flame.
With no island forest and a canopy of
tropical trees to hide under, I was able
to see what we become, what we really are.
Mummy was a quiet explosion, the hushed sound
of turning on the gas stove at the bakery. That is how she
left through the window. A quick gush of red-orange-blue
flame. Then, a streak of light slicing through the night air.
To an untrained eye, she was a glimmer
of something deceptive
in the sky. A UFO? Lightning?
The blinking lights of an airplane?
But it is just my mother—
a soucouyant, lougarou, old hag in the night.

The window above the mortar shatters as if someone
had thrown in a glass bottle filled with gasoline—
like how the island people start riots back home.

I fall to the floor and hit my face on the hardwood.
I don't even bother to get up as Mummy's hot firelight
sweeps over me and circles the apartment
before landing in the mortar—

I keep my face down and shut my eyes. My head throbs.

Something wet slides into my mouth. Blood from my nose.
I inhale long and deep and puff out hot, angry breath—

Mummy is back in her skin. The suctioning, slurping sound
of a soucouyant slipping into its human body pulls in all
my dreams along with it. She is back in this apartment,
back to her humanness, back to being my mother.
Still, I do not move—

Next comes the pitter-patter of her bare feet running
to the bathroom, then the hissing sound of her warm body
immersing in the tub. She sighs. I can hear the quiet
rippling of the ice water—

I get up, slowly, and wipe my nose with the back of my hand.
Winds gush through the broken window, bringing in Flatbush's
noise and dust with it. I will have to clean up the
broken shards of glass. But not before I help Mummy
settle back into her mothering self—

VII

When I was little, I used to ask Mummy
about her girlhood in the Caribbean—
migrating from one island to the next.
Always running from a witch hunt—
Haiti to Jamaica; Saint Lucia to Trinidad;

Martinique to Puerto Rico;
Barbados to Saint Vincent
(our names changing with each place—
lougarou to soucoyant to chupacabra)—
in search of work, in search of souls.

"What did you do when you got to a new place?"
I asked. "Did you have to hide there, too?"

"Ah, Marisol. We do not have to hide when people
stop believing in their own stories and magic,"
Mummy said. Her voice was barely above a whisper.
"But hiding was never the dream. Freedom

will be our salvation, Mari. It is easy
to shape-shift in a country where
you are freer as a monster
than you are as a   human."

I used to believe Mummy—that we are free.
But the world is opening up to me
Even as I fly and feast and
return to my human self,
wait for the new moon and
try to live a normal life—

I am hoping for my own freedom, my own
salvation, because God answers my prayers too.

My mother forgives me for trying
to keep her away from her skin.
And I let the guilt in my belly
swell into a hunger pang. It hurts
to want something so bad,
that I would risk everything—

"I understand you are angry, Mari," she says.
"But you cannot make a home
out of the burnt hole I will leave behind.
You cannot live this soucouyant life
without your mother's flame lighting
a path for you in the sky—"

She steps out of the tub and dries with
an old T-shirt. We do not own towels.
Mummy has always looked young for her age,
and that is the benefit of being what we are—

"Tomorrow, you will take over the bakery,"
she says as she gets dressed.
"Jean-Pierre is . . . well, he is in the hospital.
And I have another job. Full time. Good pay."

I hold my breath, making sure I heard her correctly.
"A job? Good pay? Will it be enough?"

"Yes, very good pay. There will be more than enough. I understand you are a young lady and . . . I should not keep you here so isolated. I will work for both of us."

Both of us?
That night, shame becomes another layer of skin
I have to shed each month to reveal
the truth of how I feel—

I need my mother, and she needs me,
the same way we need our skins to walk
through the world as both
human   and   monster.

GENEVIEVE—

Breath

I rush down from the rooftop and
the house is dead quiet—
Kate will think that I've put the baby to sleep.

So I tiptoe into the nursery.
The night-light is shining over the empty bassinet
that says   *Elliott.*

I hold baby Elliott against my body and again,
I   inhale   deep—
taking in his soft, tiny, peaceful   energy.
Who knew that holding babies could be so satisfying?

Slowly   slowly, I put him down.
He's swaddled in layers and layers of blankets
and I'm careful not to wake him   but
he is too still.   I guess that's how babies sleep.
Like stone.

Life

I've never seen myself as a baby.
Dad doesn't have any photos.
The only thing he's ever really said
about my mother was that she was
       "magical."
One thing I love about him, though:
He doesn't lie to me. If there's something
he doesn't want me to know, or if
he's not ready to say it, he just gets quiet.

That's what the beginning of my life is like—
one long empty silence; unspoken truths
from my father.   So I fill up those
hollow spaces with my own origin story.

I was born on a beautiful island to a
mermaid.   Dad loved going to the
Caribbean. He first went as a kid with his rich
golf-playing daddy, my grandfather. The story
goes that Dad got mixed up with some weed-smoking
Rastas up in the mountains and was never the same,
which is how he fell in love with other people's cultures;
which is how he fell in love with a mermaid, maybe—

my mother.   She was born under the ocean—
a dark-skinned woman with gorgeous
iridescent fins and a huge afro.

                    Maybe, I am half mermaid.
My hair becomes a billion shrunken ringlets
when it's wet, and turns into a giant afro when
it's dry. My skin is slowly becoming
fish scales—flaking and itching and—

I've never been to the Caribbean.
Sometimes I wonder if swimming
in the ocean would help, but—

I did that once when I was a little girl,
and it was painful. It couldn't have been the ocean.
Maybe it was a bad sunburn. If my mother is from the ocean,
        then why would it hurt so bad to swim in it?

Dad has never denied the story I made up about myself.
"That's how myth is born," he'd said.
"The stories we tell ourselves can be
            just as powerful as the truth."

So my father read me fables about the
West African Mami Wata, and the
        Caribbean La Siren.

The thing about stories, the thing about myths
is that with each new truth, the gods,
goddesses, monsters, and creatures
become part of a beautiful
exquisite corpse—   like me.

I am a half mermaid whose skin
is made from silk that burns
at night under a full
moon, and then
I turn into a
moth and
fly—

like a chimera.

My father's stories
        help me make sense
                of my changing body.

II

Finally, at sunrise, I sleep deep
without any nightmares—

And my skin is calm.
But Kate is not. She

screams from down the hall
and I want to stay in bed so bad

because only a sliver of morning
light is coming into my room.
But my stepmother is crying.
        Not the babies.

I want to care, but I am finally,
finally without pain. My alarm clock
goes off just as Kate yells at Dad
                to call an ambulance.

My heart stops.

III

Bethany is crying, but Elliott is not.
Bethany is moving, but Elliott is not.
Bethany is breathing, but Elliott is not.

Kate is crying, but my father is not—

"He's so cold, he's so cold, he's so cold,"
    Kate keeps saying over and over again
as she rocks him in her arms and—

He was hot when I put him down, or
      was it me?
He was sleeping when I put him down, or
      was he not?

He was as still as stone, or—

That stone sinks deep in my belly
and my skin crawls, but it's not from
heat or pain, but from something else, like—

"What happened to him?" I ask groggily.
Then the tears fall because maybe I already
know the answer. Dad comes to me holding
      Bethany.

"Sweetie, we need you right now," he says,
his voice shaking, his eyes red, his hair disheveled—
"Hold her while we take care of Elliott."

I shake my head no.

"She's fine, Gen. Just take her. We need you right now."

Then Kate unravels—dropping to her knees with
      Elliott in her arms and sobbing.
"Daniel, should we go? Should we take him?"

"They'll be here faster than we can get there, honey,"
Dad says, and keeps holding Bethany out to me—

"No," I whisper, remembering how Elliott felt in my arms
and I don't want—

"Genevieve!" Dad raises his voice. "Hold the baby!"

"No! No!" I cry out, backing away.

Dad's eyes well up with tears and this hurts—
 This hurts so bad. More than my skin.
 More than anything, and I don't know why.

And I become small,   small.
Smaller than the newborn twins.
Smaller than Elliott in Kate's arms—

IV

I used to take up so much space—
Dad never let me doubt that I was his number one.
  I mattered more to him than Kate.

Even on the day she announced
that she was pregnant, Dad came
to check in on me to ask how I felt.

I wanted siblings—

And they were born.
And they filled up the house
with their tiny presence.
Two of them, at once.

There was no time for Dad to check in on me.
There was no room for my complaints
and my tantrums, and my   feelings.
"So   many   *feelings*," Dad would
always joke, letting me know that I was a
teenager and my emotions were normal
and this culture has no rites of passage to
usher me into adulthood—

And he always turns my feelings into some
scholarly article—
Everything about me
is a textbook, a case study, a dissertation,
an anthropological theory—

      Even my skin.
"You know, in Caribbean folklore,"
Dad told me one night when I first
started getting these rashes,
"the soucouyant or the lougarou shed

their skin at night and flew around feeding
on the souls of babies—"

"Dad, that's horrible! Please, no more stories!"
I'd said, and playfully pushed him out of my room.

Since the babies, he's stopped telling me stories,
he's stopped checking in, and—
Now I'm supposed to just hold the baby?

V

Sirens and lights flood
our tree-lined street, and police cars
usually pass our Prospect Lefferts Gardens
neighborhood to head straight for
Flatbush or Crown Heights.
So I know the neighbors will be
watching from their windows.

Dad had put Bethany down
in her car seat on the parlor floor.
He tries to do CPR on Elliott
and so does Kate, pressing two fingers
on his little chest, but he is so tiny and
fragile and I swear this is the saddest
thing I've ever seen. My face is wet

with an ocean of tears. The salt stings my skin.
And my guilt fills this entire house like thick smoke.

I'm the only one who hasn't
tried to breathe life back into the baby—
because I swear, maybe, I was
the one who'd taken his breath away.

I believe in all the stories Dad has told me
about magical creatures, old women mostly,
who eat the souls of babies at night.
I believe in changelings and Baba Yaga stories.

When you're raised on folklore and fairy tales,
possibilities are infinite.   The lines between
reality and fantasy are blurred—

The doorbell rings and the least
I can do is rush over to let the
paramedics in—
But it's not the people wearing
uniforms and medical equipment
who greet me—

A woman is standing there with just
a summer dress and a too-bright smile.
    She must be cold.

"Wrong house," I tell her through quiet sobs.

"No, no, no! Come in, come in!"
Kate calls out from inside, motioning
for the woman to move past me.

The paramedics are trying to double-park
on our narrow street and I wave them over
to the front of our brownstone.

But there's more commotion from inside
the house as that new woman tries to pry
the baby away from Kate.

Kate finally releases Elliott to this strange
lady and Bethany starts crying and Dad
goes over to pick her up and the paramedics
are running towards the house and my insides
are a tsunami of emotions—

The woman with no coat on just walked into our house
and is holding my baby brother who isn't breathing
and I want to stop her but the paramedics
    rush in and I point to her and—

She   doesn't let   him   go.

The paramedics are reaching for Elliott
but the strange woman still has him
in her arms and her lips are moving like
she's praying—

"What are you doing?" I yell.

But Dad is holding Bethany and he's staring
like his eyes are stuck on this lady—

"Dad! What is she doing?" I yell again.

And—

Baby Elliott starts
            coughing   and
                                crying.

The paramedic finally takes him from the
woman and—   and—
my breath is stuck in my chest and I'm
just standing there, staring   like Dad.

Kate yelps and rushes to Elliott,
but the paramedic is checking his vitals.
"He wasn't breathing! He wasn't breathing!"
            Kate shouts.

"He's fine, ma'am. He's fine," the medic says.

And now, both Bethany and Elliott are crying
and it's music—

Kate is holding Elliott again and she's trying to
convince the paramedics that her sweet baby boy
wasn't breathing, wasn't moving, and was cold,
so, so cold—

Dad is nodding, shaking his head, staring,
and frozen all at the same time,   like me.

Kate never says the word   *dead*.

The paramedics ask if Kate and Dad
would like them to take Elliott in—

But that strange woman says, "Sometimes,
they sleep so deep . . . we cannot even tell."

The whole room goes quiet, like—

"Who the fuck is this lady?"
I ask out loud. I didn't mean to, but
it's the first full sentence I say
because she is the only thing that
doesn't make sense right now—

Dad shoots me a look, but there are
far worse things right now than me
dropping an f-bomb.

So he ignores me as the lady goes over to
Kate and has her open up her nightgown
so Elliott can rest on her bare skin—

"Skin to skin. He must know that you
are living and breathing, too, so that he
can live and   breathe," she says
        with a thick accent.

"Oh, this is, um . . . ," Kate starts, finally exhaling.

"Lourdes," the woman says, making a long, heavy
O sound like the word *mood*.

"Yes, yes. Lourdes is here to . . . ," Kate sighs deep,
mispronouncing the woman's name as Lor-Dees.
"She's here to help. She's here to help."
She cuts her eyes at Dad as if he's been
proven wrong.

Is this the help that Kate hired? The one with no
interview, background check, or references?
I wonder.

Finally Kate sits on the couch and starts
nursing Elliott, and it's as if my tiny sibling
was just   born again.
The woman—Lourdes—helps Bethany latch,
too, and this is the first time that my stepmother,
my dad, my twin siblings are all quiet, calm, and
                    breathing—

VI

I let the paramedics out and I'm still
                    holding my breath—
I'm standing there looking at this woman
who doesn't have on a coat and whose deep
brown skin is so smooth, so bright, I swear
she's not from here   and I'm still
                    holding my breath—
School starts in a couple of hours and Micah
is supposed to come by and I'm still
                    holding my breath—
My baby brother died or almost died and
I don't know what the fuck just happened so
                    I'm still
                    holding my breath—
I go to the kitchen to make some tea
and maybe breakfast and I'm still sleepy and
                    holding my breath—

Then that new woman comes in, still smiling,
staring, bright-eyed, and she looks so familiar.
          "Have you been here before?" I ask.

She looks at me—   just looks at me.
I turn away because her eyes are digging
into me and I don't know who this lady is.

"Are you, like, the new nanny or au pair
          or whatever?" I ask.

Her eyes are glistening. Are those tears?

"I gotta get the fuck outta here," I say
and leave the kitchen, brushing past her
and then   my entire skin goes hot
     and I hiss—

I stare at Lourdes as if she made this happen.
Our eyes meet and she reaches out and touches
my arm—   Coolness. Calmness.
And I let out a deep, long   breath—
I close my eyes and settle into this peacefulness.

              I am   breathing—

"Who   are   you?" I ask.

She smiles and a single tear rolls down her cheek,
against her smooth, clear,   dark brown skin.
"Genevieve," she says, pronouncing my name in French
and it rolls off her tongue so fluidly, like water.
Like an ocean wave—

         "Yes?" I ask.
In that moment, I notice the shape of her eyes,
the fullness of her cheeks, her plump lips,
and her small halo of an afro—

"Who   are   you?"
I ask again.

Dad comes into the kitchen, and his eyes
only land on this lady. "Lourdes," he says,
exactly the way the woman pronounces it.
Her name rolls off his tongue so fluidly, like water.
Like an ocean wave—

—MARISOL

Work

A long string of tiny bells hangs
from the front door of the bakery.
So every time someone comes in, it is
an alarm for me to rush to the counter
and ask, "How may I help you?"

I place my hand over my heart the way
I learned to do at the resorts—
I am always in service
to the tourists.

Except here, the people who buy
bread are workers like me—
island people who want a
taste of home.

Hard dough, coco bread, hops bread,
spiced bun, fried bake, coconut bake,
bulla cake, bammy, roti,
bread pudding, patties,
pholourie—

But today, we are down to two kinds
of bread and I have to keep saying,

"I don't know when we will have more."

They say that Jean-Pierre has been
in the hospital breathing through
a tube and his wife has not left his side.
So he has not come in to pay his
workers. And the workers will not be
baking until he does.
It is all my fault.

They say that work in this city is
as if the sun never goes down.
There are day shifts and night shifts,
and the streets are full of
tired, lifeless zombies.
Lougarou can never become zombies.
As long as there is a sun, moon, and sky;
fire, water, and skin;
we will never be lifeless.
So we will always have to work.
Mummy went out to find more work.
It is all my fault.

"Here, you must learn to shed another layer of skin.
The skin that is given to you by them:
Black, girl, poor, and immigrant—
Wear the skin that is given to you by your foremothers:
powerful, cosmic, and   incomprehensible,"

Mummy had said when we first arrived
that cold evening last month in December.

Now I am just wearing the skin given to me by them.
Mummy has not yet returned to remind me of
the skin she gave to me.
It is all my fault.

Where is she?
Why hasn't she come back?
Is this what she
meant by full-time work?
That she would be gone for days?

Even at the resorts on the islands, we came home.
We could not be greedy with the work.
There was always someone else who   needed
the hours, the tips, the pay, the job—
and because of that, we had time and space
to breath in life—

Here, work is the life,
and life is the work.

II

For the third time today, a customer asks,
"Shouldn't you be in school?"

Even at fifteen, I don't look my age.
I have the face of a little girl,
and Mummy looks like my big sister.

"Today is a holiday," I say,
without knowing what the holidays are here.
I can't keep up this lie.
We are supposed to be hiding.
And yes, I am supposed to be in school.

I've been absent from school
on days like this, when Mummy wanders
the night sky looking for life;
when Mummy wanders the day streets
looking for more work—

I take her place here at the bakery,
making sure that whatever few dollars
Jean-Pierre's wife pays us stays in our purses.
No time for idleness. No time for school.

On the islands, we worked to go to
school. We have to pay to learn.
We pay for books, uniforms, and even
for the van or motorbike that will
take us to school.

"It's free, you know?" the customer says.
"Public school. It's not like back home.
Good education here is as free as the wind."

I want to tell her that this is not true.
Everything of value comes with a price.
I, of all people, know that money is not
the only exchange for the things we need.

III

Before the bakery closes for the night,
one of the workers comes to me with
her hand out. I have been at the
register all day only because
this was Mummy's job.

"I've tried to call Jean-Pierre and his wife,"
she pleads. "It's been two weeks since
I've been paid. Please, I need to
put food on the table," she says.

She is older than Mummy. She keeps a fishnet
bonnet over her hair, and the blue apron with
Island Bakery embroidered across the chest
is stained with flour and oil.

So I open the cash register and
give her a wad   of twenty-dollar bills.

There is a boy who mops, sweeps, and cleans
the kitchen. He hides in the back and only
comes out when it is time to close.
He has secrets behind his eyes, so
we barely look at each other.
I give him his space, and
I give him money too.

Then I close out the register,
wrap the rest of the coconut bake
to take with me upstairs,
and turn off the lights.

Our apartment is a freezer.
Light snow blows in through the
shattered window and
I look for Mummy in the sky,
even though it is not her time
to shape-shift and fly.

Jean-Pierre is not around to
make us pay for the damage.
Jean-Pierre is not around to
also fix the damage.

I wear every piece of clothing
I own and wrap myself
in the old blanket both
me and Mummy sleep on.
I sit by the door and pray
for my mother's safe return
while breaking off only a small
piece of the bake—

My stomach rumbles,
from hunger and from   guilt.
How could I be so stupid, thinking that
I could get rid of my mother?

At the very least, when Mummy comes
home tonight, she will have
a little something to eat.

GENEVIEVE——

Work

The house is the quietest it's ever been
since the twins came home.
So silence is my lullaby, even though
it's morning and I should be going to school.

Except a bunch of pots and pans are causing
a racket in the kitchen and that's an unusual sound
in this house. Kate doesn't like cooking. Dad thinks
he's a home chef. But still, we live off deliveries
and takeouts from local restaurants, even though
there's a long list of foods I can't eat.

Thirty minutes until I'm supposed to leave for
school, but my brain feels like it's floating
in syrup. My eyes hurt. My body is aching.
And my skin is   normal.
Finally!   Thank goodness.
Except, my face still breaks out, but still—

Don't come. Everything is a mess right now,
I text Micah.   *I'm not going to school today.*

I put down the phone before he even responds,
and check in on Dad and Kate to make

sure they're not dead—that's how hard they're
sleeping. The twins' bassinets are pushed up
against the sides of their bed, and last night's chaos
knocked the shit out of everybody, except me.

The strange lady is still here, taking over our
kitchen, and I watch her closely. She's watching
me too. Her eyes are studying me as if
I'm one of the twins—checking to see if I'm
            still breathing.

"You can leave now," I tell her. "I'll be
staying home today. So when the twins wake up . . ."

When the twins wake up, I don't want to hold them.
            I can't hold them—

Lourdes doesn't say anything and is washing the
dishes by hand even though we have a dishwasher.
She knows where everything is, and I believe
Dad when he said she was one of the cleaning ladies.
I've never seen her before. And she knew my name.

On Saturdays, the house is always sparkling when
I come home from dance class. The four floors are dust-
and allergen-free. And before the twins came, Kate hired
a whole team of people to do a deep clean.

And maybe Lourdes was one of them—
         but we've never had a maid or a nanny.
         Dad took care of me since I was a baby.

"You can leave now," I repeat, because it always
felt wrong to have a Black woman clean our house.
So I feel some type of way having her here, taking
care of the twins while Kate bosses her around—

Lourdes smiles, holds her chin up, and says,
"This is my job. I work here now."
Her accent makes every word a song.
Almost like   a lullaby.

II

My eyelids get heavy as I watch her
clean every corner of the already
spotless kitchen—
On the couch near the kitchen,
I take a nap, and I sleep so good.
Deep, deep REM sleep where
         every cell is rejuvenated.
Especially my skin. And my silk pajamas
feel even softer against my body. Warmth
washes over my face and I open my
eyes to bright white-yellow sunshine—

It's summer!   It's summer?

No. We're on vacation. And Dad
finally agreed to take us to the
Caribbean, because outside the
window is a turquoise ocean
reaching far into the distance
to touch the clear blue sky.

I turn to look for a door,
and the white-sand beach is
already there to greet me.

And there she is—
without me even looking for her.
An afro surfaces, bobbing in the waves.
I can't make out her features—
Her face is a brown shimmering blur.

"Dad, is that her?" I ask, but I look
up at the sun as if my father lives
in the clouds—

The mermaid—my mother, maybe—
propels her half-human, half-fish self up
out of the water, arching her body like a
dolphin, reaching towards the sky,
the clouds, the sun—my father.

Is this how I was born?

I walk to where the waves crash
along the shore; the cool ocean
    kisses my bare feet,
except I can't feel anything.
No pain, no heat, no warm breeze.
    Nothing.
And then,   darkness eases
towards the edge of the sky,
creeping over this island like
a ghost—   A bad sign?

Please, God. Don't let this be
another nightmare—
let this be   *a dream.*

So the moon rises—
the bright, white, shining moon
       chases the sun away.

And the ocean—
the ocean retreats, runs from the
shore as if I'm the one chasing it;
as if I'm the one that makes it hurt.

And the moon—
it's closer now. Its craters become round eyes,

a broad nose, and full lips like mine—
And the moon

      becomes a face;

  a smile;

    a soft voice.
"Mama," I whisper in my dream,

  just as a flaming meteor dashes across—

"Genevieve," someone whispers.
And the moon   is her—

I sit up on the couch.
Lourdes is staring down at me,
her face is way too close to mine.
I scoot back to the corner of the couch
trying to get away.

Her entire presence feels warm.

      Hot, even.

"You were having a fever dream," she whispers.
"Breakfast is ready."

III

Dad and Kate come down
each holding a twin,

and I crank my neck trying to
see their little faces.

The entire brownstone smells like

a   home. And I'm afraid to look
at the spread covering the dining
table.   There's so much stuff
                        I can't eat.

"Lor-Dees!" Kate sings. "You've outdone
yourself! This looks delicious." She's holding
Elliott. I can tell by the blue blanket, and his
matching little blue eyes are wide open.

I whisper, "Thank you, God."

But Dad still looks like he hasn't slept.
He stares at the food. Then our eyes meet, and he
doesn't say anything about me not being in school.
Thank goodness. "Oh, um. Gen is allergic to . . . ,"
he starts to say.

"No, no, no," Lourdes says. "It's good food.
Good for the, uh . . ." She rubs the back of her
hand, and she already knows that something's
wrong with my skin. Hers is smooth, too smooth.

Like, she seems old, around Dad and Kate's age.
But her skin—

"I have a gluten allergy, maybe. I can't have too
much sugar. I don't know. My skin breaks out
randomly, so it can be just about everything
on this table," I say, rambling. My stomach growls.

"Lourdes, you really didn't have to . . ."
Dad says, and he's   so pale.
His eyes are moving about as if he can't make
sense of anything right now—the twins,
the food, last night, and, maybe, this lady.

Dad and Kate place the babies in their bassinets
and sit around the table to inhale
the food as if they haven't eaten in days.

"We have salt fish and bake, fried plantain,
cornmeal porridge, smoke herring and okra stew,
dumplings, and boiled egg. . . ." Lourdes sings each
word as if this entire meal is a performance.

And I eat too. Picking at everything and waiting
for some kind of reaction. Nothing happens.
I didn't know that I could be so   ravenous.
I devour the bread. Fried bake, she calls it.
        I take spoonfuls of the salt fish.

Nothing happens.
And all that island food fills me up
         like a big, warm hug from something
I've been missing my whole life.

"Daniel," Kate says in between mouthfuls.
"This reminds me of our wedding.
It's like we're at the Hibiscus Resort again,
except without the ocean and warm weather."

"Lor-Dees," she continues, still mispronouncing
her name. "Please stay. We have a guest
room upstairs, fully furnished. We'll
double the pay and . . ."

"Kate," Dad interrupts. "Shouldn't we . . ."

Kate puts her hand up to stop Dad from speaking.
"Please, Lor-Dees. I insist."

"It's Lourdes," Dad says. "Like . . . the Louvre.
It's French, honey."

"French like Genevieve," I say, pronouncing
my name the way the lady did, the way my dad
did when I was little, until I asked him not to.
What good is the French pronunciation of my
name when I don't even know

the mother who named me?
"Oh, yes! *Lourdes* speaks French!"
Kate says. "*Lourdes*, you can teach the twins
some French, and soon they'll develop their
palate for these island flavors!"

The twins start fidgeting at the same time
and Lourdes comes to the rescue,
taking Elliott from his bassinet. Dad picks
up Bethany and holds her against his chest as
he's looking at Lourdes,
       but not looking at Lourdes.
Like, he's trying not to see her, but she's there
        rocking Elliott and staring at *him*.

"I can draft a contract, so that we're on the same
page," Kate continues. "I'll have a binder for you
detailing your job description and . . ."

"Kate, we don't need to . . . ," Dad starts.

"We've talked about this. We need a nanny.
She's here. We found our person!"

"Is she my nanny too?" I ask, being unserious
to lighten the mood a bit.
I glance at Lourdes, who is pretending
to not hear us as she rocks baby Elliott—

"Huh, we could've used a nanny when
you were little. You were a handful,"
Kate says, half laughing, half serious.

Dad shifts in his seat as if Kate just said
the worst thing to him, and I catch him
glancing at Lourdes, whose face goes sour,
like this was an insult to her too.

"Yes!" Lourdes suddenly says, and we're all startled.
"Yes, I will work for you all the time! I can stay here
to help take care of the twins, Elliott and Bethany.
I can . . . I will . . . I will live here too."

Her singsong voice trails off, as if she's thinking
twice about her decision. And she stares at me
        as if she's here
                to take care
                        of me too.

"Thank you!" Kate whispers, and then sighs
like she's relieved, like she just hired a clone—
except Lourdes is the opposite of her in every way.
"Daniel can take you to get your things.
You'll have your own linen and towels. I'll get you
whatever else you need. We're just
happy to have you here."

And I catch Lourdes glancing at my father again,
as if they're exchanging quiet, secret words.
She pleads with her eyes. He blinks and looks
away. And it's almost as if they already know
each other. But I push that feeling down because

I haven't slept and the lines between
my nightmares and reality are blurred now—

—MARISOL

School

Mummy used to have a cell phone.
Then it got stolen and she vowed never to
own anything that people would want to steal.
Then I reminded her of the mortar and
how some of the people back home
wanted to rid the island of old magic,
ancient power. They would steal our mortars
to sell to scientists, to sell as souvenirs—

"It was already stolen," she had said.
"Then I got it back."

I don't ask my mother many questions.
She hides her secrets in her fireblood;
takes them with her to the night sky,
prays to everything more powerful than us,
and asks for forgiveness
after she enacts revenge—

Maybe she has waged a war on someone
and it will take nights and nights to
destroy their entire lineage.

"Who hurt you, Mummy?
Let me fight for you too,"

I say to the morning sky as the
sun rises and casts a dim light
into our empty apartment.

Mummy still has not come home
and neither of us has a phone
to reach the other.

This is not the first time she has
abandoned me like this.
But this is the first time she has left me
all alone with no village of other
soucouyant or lougarou
near and far to keep me company.

A truck stops in front of the bakery
and I should be downstairs
to greet the men delivering flour
and other supplies. But this is not
my job. No one is here to do
the work that Jean-Pierre left behind.
This is still my fault—

Some people walk by to see that the
store is closed. But the boy who cleans the
kitchen is standing outside because, maybe,
he will not be able to find another job.

He is quiet like me,
so I don't know his name.
He looks my age. And maybe he has magic
hidden beneath the surface of his oil-black skin.
I've seen his kind before on the islands.
The tourists love them. Dark. Strong. Mysterious.
Dangerous. Not to us, but to them. Still, I am careful.
Still, we do not ask
and we   do not tell
other Caribbean newcomers about our magic.

So I stick my head out the glassless window
and shout, "Hey! You should be in school!"

He looks up and smiles bright.
His teeth are immaculate. His smile is holy.
A dangerous thing for me—

Downstairs, I unlock the door to the building
to let him in. He rushes past me and goes
straight to the kitchen in the back.
A black cat follows him in, but it is too
quick for me to stop it—

because on the islands, a black cat
is not just an omen, it can be a hiding place
for a soul.

"We are closed today," I tell him.
"And no cats in the bakery!"

He doesn't say anything, opens
a bag of old coco bread and takes one.
The cat has disappeared to some
hidden corner of the bakery.
The boy sits on the counter and starts
eating. He does not have to
explain. Work is where he eats.
For me, work is where I sleep.

"You should be in school too,"
he finally says with a mouthful of bread.
"But people like us have to hide.
We have to stick together."
His jawline is chiseled stone.
His face is a sculpture.

Something stirs in my belly
and it's not hunger—
I've felt like this before,
but only for the tourist boys
from America, whose presence
at the resorts was always like
fresh fallen snow on a hot island.

Still, I do not ask. And I do not tell.
I don't even search his eyes for
what kind of monster he is.

"My name is Marisol," I say.

"I know," he says. "I'm Jaden."
His voice is the rumbling sky
before a thunderstorm.

And maybe, I have found a
magical kin in Jaden.

II

Someone bangs on the door and the bells chime.
There is a short line of customers and they
want to buy whatever crumbs we have left.

"What should we do?" I ask Jaden.

He walks to the door and
points to the *Closed* sign.

The familiar customers curse us through
the glass door and ask what happened to
Jean-Pierre and his wife; and they say

that this business has been here for years
and they have been loyal and will be
getting their bread from elsewhere.
Then they finally leave.

"I hear he's going to die," Jaden says,
still with his mouth full of bread.

My belly sinks with the weight of
useless guilt. "No he is not," I say.

"I wonder who pissed him off."

"Why do you ask that? He was just sick."

"I don't believe it. All kinds of spirits
were always coming after Jean-Pierre."

"Have *you* gone after him?" I ask.

"Not yet," he says. "I need this job."

"So you will work here forever?
What kind of American dream is that?"

"I didn't come here to dream. I came here to live.
And you? Why did you leave the islands?"

"I did not come here to live. I came here to dream,"
I say, without giving it much thought because
no one has ever asked me that question,
and it was not my choice to come here.

"So why aren't you out there dreaming?"
Jaden asks, stepping closer to me.
His accent is not as thick as mine,
and I wonder how long he has been
away from home.

"Because I dream . . .   at night."

"You've never heard of daydreaming, Marisol?"
He laughs. His short dreadlocks reach down
to his chin, and when he speaks,
I catch a glimpse of his bloodred tongue—

I know what he is!

I step back away from him, because
the red-tongued jab jab is forbidden.
I search his dreads for the horns,
but they are well hidden.
The stirring in my belly
is now simmering. A sign of danger
or something else?

Jab jab like Jaden are fearsome—
with the magical ability to
steal the souls of their victims.
But to us magical girls, jab jab are enticing.

He says he has come here to live, but I don't ask
him *how* he lives—

III

The streets are alive now, and I can watch
from outside the door instead of the
apartment window.

The kids my age are even closer—
so close, I can sniff their energy
through the cold glass.
I should be with them now.

"What's it like?" Jaden asks.
"Walking to school like an
aimless zombie. Sitting in those
classrooms like an empty
coconut shell. They fill you up
with ideas that make you even
less   human."

I scowl at him and kiss my teeth.
"You sound like a yardie. A vagabond.
You could've stayed on whatever island
you flew away from."

"You think this life is better, don't you?"
he asks, stepping closer to stand
next to me by the door.

I move away again. He can sense the
dormant flames beneath my skin.
And I can sense mischief on his breath.
He looks like midnight, his dark skin
speckled with starlight—
He smells like hot iron forged
with fire like mine.
He is ancient magic too.
On the islands, his secret self
only emerges during carnival.
But here,   he is free to roam
the night in search of   prey.
Like me.

"This life is only better
if we exist as only human," I say.

"Better for us or for them?"
He points with his bottom lip
to the other people walking
the sidewalks. Except here,
they're not tourists, they're not
visitors, even. And I wonder
how long this neighborhood
has been called Little Caribbean
with all the tourists who are not tourists.

I'm supposed to start my second week
of school today, but Mummy has not
bought me a backpack and new clothes
for me to look decent for the teachers.

Those kids' backpacks are slung over their
shoulders carelessly. Some are even
wearing plastic sandals, as if they are
going to an icy beach somewhere.

Someone knocks on the door again.
They ask if we are open and Jaden
has to keep pointing to the sign.
After they leave, I step out
to inhale the cold morning air.
I cough and sneeze.

"Be careful now," Jaden says.
"Freezing temperatures are not good
for lungs made of fire."

And he already knows what I am.
"You be careful," I say.
"Just because the city lights are on
all night doesn't mean it's carnival.
You can't play mas every night, Jab Jab."

He laughs an evil laugh,
opening his mouth wide to
let me see his red tongue.
Slowly, the tips of his horns
poke out of his dreadlocks.
Then they quickly retreat and
he stops laughing.

He comes closer and touches
my cheek with the back of his hand.
"I've always liked the skin of soucouyant.
So smooth and pretty."

I push his hand away and say,
"On the islands, the worst love stories
are between magic and mischief.
Jab jab always prefer the tourists.

125

And the tourists always prefer us.
To kiss a red-tongued devil will only
fuel our flames—and you know it."

"We're not on the islands anymore, Marisol,"
he says, almost hissing, as if asking for a kiss.

The simmering inside of me comes to a boil.
I cannot stay with him here,   alone.
At least with customers, we are distracted
from each other. In an empty store with
no adults around, we will become curious.

So I inhale a deep cooling breath
and turn away from him. *Forget him
and forget home.* I don't need anyone
else keeping me chained to old magic.

So this is my chance to daydream
and start my second week of school—

Mummy is out there living the life she
wanted for herself. And I am supposed
to just wait for her? My entire life
reduced to eating from this bakery
and sleeping on a cold floor?

And longing for a boy I can't kiss?

I had learned to dream when I used
to clean the rooms at the resorts—
covering the cloud-soft mattresses
with bleached linen;
folding expensive swimsuits
and dresses; serving the people who
come to our islands to escape whatever
monstrosities are out there in the world—

monstrosities they helped to create.
And I am a monster too—

So I go to the cash register and
take what is left—

"You're not scared that someone or
something will come after you for stealing?"
Jaden asks, nibbling on another piece of bread
with a menacing smile.

"I am taking what has been owed to us.
You have your bread, I have my money."
So I step out of the bakery wearing just
a sweatshirt and jeans. I need to go
back to school. Back to the dream
to escape my life of being a
nightmare—

My mother will always find me
because fire catches fire, always.

IV

On the islands, the children who go to
school and the children who go to
work part ways at a fork in the road.

Them with their plaid uniforms
and starch-white shirts, and us
with our polo shirts or dresses
branded with a hotel's logo.

Today, in this new country,
at this new crossroads, maybe,
my magical life can end so
my normal life can begin.

I follow my friends (who do not
know they are my friends)
all the way down Flatbush Avenue
as they laugh and talk and live free,
and I am one of them   for now.

Across the street is the castle of a building
with a giant American flag dancing

in the cold wind.
My school—

A group of girls walk huddled together
like birds under a rain-soaked tree.
The way they talk, giggle, and seem to float
reminds me of my friends back on the islands.
I miss them bad. So, so bad—

The kids are crowding into the school
like a carnival mas camp behind the
big trucks on the road. Except there is no
sea of colorful costumes and no soca music
blasting out of giant speakers.

And I am always invisible—
No one notices my old sweatshirt and worn jeans.
No one notices my plump body, my round face with
thick lips and a wide nose, my short kinky hair,
and my dark, dark skin—

All the things that made me invisible
in the resorts too. Easing in and out of
the tourists' way so I don't obstruct
their view of our ocean—

I try to do the same here, on the busy streets

as people go to work and school, but I am
still a body taking up space—

They push me—from behind and
from the side, urging me to get closer and
closer to this majestic building with
its tall and wide steps and crimson
doors and prisonlike windows
and uniformed men
guarding the
entrance.

One of the girls turns around to
see me staring at them—

She cuts her eyes at me and kisses her teeth,
just like they do on the islands—*STEUPS*.

The familiar sound makes me smile a little.

Then all four of them turn
and before they say anything—

"Move, you ugly bitch!"
a boy says out loud, and bumps me
hard, making me fall to the ground.
I hit my chin on the concrete, and I
bite down on my tongue and the pain—

my head, my ears . . .   everything pounds.

                    Someone says something to the boy,
                    but not enough for him to say sorry.

And they laugh   and laugh   and laugh—

            I peek up to see a girl stepping around me—
her long, thin leg crossing over the threshold that is
my body as if I am just a fallen log in a rainforest.
            She holds that boy's hand and together
                        they walk up the stairs.

                            I can't see his face.
                            I need to see his face.

Heat   heat   heat
            rises   to the surface
                                    of my skin—
            And   this is when I want
                to become   a monster.

                    But time will force me to wait
            for sweet   sweet vengeance.
            A burning rage   settles in my core—

GENEVIEVE—

School

I didn't even catch up on homework
last night, too busy helping with the twins.
(But if I'm being honest, I was watching
    the new nanny too.)
They were calm and happy, and Elliott
    smiled for the first time! Bethany
has an attitude and we're going to be besties.
It's like that lady's presence is what
the twins needed all along—

Or maybe Kate is less stressed
now that she's getting help and the
twins are picking up on her calm energy.

    And Dad—
is acting weird.   Kate is mad that he didn't
take paternity leave and I think he just wants to
escape to his classes and his books and his research
       and everything is chill
for, like, one day.   Except

II

Lourdes is in every corner of the house
watching me, just watching me, and

I can't wait to get back to school.

This morning, my skin feels   fine.
But my face still looks like shit.
        Cystic acne—
and it's been   pure hell
living with it these past few years.

I can't even cover it with makeup
'cause it'll make it worse.
Hypoallergenic, noncomedogenic—
nothing works.
So I let my thick, curly hair hang
over my cheeks and forehead and
it distracts people from my face because
my hair—   my body—   my dancing—
all pull attention away from   my skin—

This morning, my soul feels   rested.
But my insides are a whirl of feelings
I can't place.   Just weird energy—
And Kate gave Lourdes the guest room on the
top floor and she has to pass my room on her way
downstairs,   and I swear she's like a fucking
ghost the way she pops up from out of nowhere.
        I'm not used to her being here—

This morning she's on our floor with a duster,
        a broom, and a mop.
And what the actual fuck! This place is already clean!

Lourdes is in the hallway passing her finger
along the banister, checking for dust
(still wearing that summer dress in winter).
I swear she's just trying to find stuff to clean.

Then she turns around and catches me looking
at her through the crack in my door.
I quickly turn away to face the mirror.
But   but   instead of seeing myself,
it's Lourdes staring back at me. I blink and blink
        and blink until—

III

"I have something for you," she says from the hall,
"Something for your . . ." She rubs her cheeks.

Part of me wants to slam the door shut in her face,
        but I just look back into the mirror
to check my own cheeks, my own eyes, my own face.

        The way she smiles—
        The way her eyes widen—

The way her thick lips curve up—
The way she looks at me—

Lourdes pushes the door open and comes in.

"Oh, you don't have to clean my bedroom.
I got it," I say, rushing to push her out.

But she reaches and touches my face.
It happens so quickly that I don't even pull
back. I let her warm hand rest on my cheek,
and it becomes cool.
                    Then cold.

I close my eyes and my skin suddenly feels like
it's actually   actually becoming silk
                under her touch—

I open my eyes and jolt back.
"What did you do?" I ask, and my words are
        smoke escaping my mouth—

I look at her hands but they're empty.
Her eyes are welling up with tears.

"Get out," I say, whispering at first. Then I shout,
        "Get out!"

No one hears me. No one hears me yelling at
the new nanny who just touched my skin and
made me feel like   like—

Her smile deflates like I just   crushed her soul
or something.   She leaves and I don't feel bad.

I'm in the mirror again,   slowly
slowly   the   nodules and pustules
level   extinguish
like tiny volcanoes cooling; lava receding—

A war has been raging on my skin and
everything that's been erupting on my face
has surrendered to this woman's touch—

I lean into the mirror, my own eyes watering.
My skin glows like embers,   like stars.
And I stare for a long second before reaching
for my vanity bag.   It's been a habit—

buying products and makeup for the day when
my skin clears—   for this day.

A surge of energy rushes through me
and I feverishly dig into the bag for a
new bottle of moisturizer primer
concealer   liquid foundation

bronzer   blush
eye shadow in three different shades
(stardust   midnight   ghost).

Highlight for my cheekbones and the tip of my nose.
     Liner. Falsies. Mascara.
I try on five different shades of lipstick.
I settle for   a gloss that makes
my lips look like glass.

I step back and take a good look at myself.
I don't even know if I did this right.
Rena and Trish let me practice on them
because if I let even a foundation brush
touch my skin I'd break out in boils.

But now   and now
Nothing.   Just my face.
          My clear
          pretty face.

IV

"Wow!" is the first thing Micah says
when I step outside the brownstone.
He's standing at the bottom of the steps
looking up at me as if I'm all dressed up
for the prom or something.

Except it's Wednesday in the middle of
January and senior prom is five months away.
And I'm just wearing black leggings and
my black puffer coat.

The sun is bright
and so is Micah's smile.
I like him when he's like this.
Gentle and vulnerable. Like, he can be
really nice when he wants to. Or just
when he thinks he has the prettiest girl
in the world. That's how he makes me
feel when he looks at me like this.

Micah isn't bad looking either. I mean,
it's better if a boy likes you more than
you like him. He keeps his sides faded
and his short braids shiny and fresh.
His dark skin is like the night against mine.
And I love the way he smells—
I could inhale him like a meal.

I stand on the second-to-last step
so that we're eye-to-eye, face-to-face
and I'm not hiding anymore.
I need him to see that it all went away
and my face is like his smile and
the morning sky—clear, dewy, and bright.

I wrap my arms around his neck and try
to kiss him, but he's stuck on my face.

"You look . . . I mean . . . you always been
a baddie, but now . . . ," he says, trying to find
the right words 'cause I know he doesn't want
to say it: I look better now that my skin is clear.

He finally kisses me and my hair blows in the
wind, enveloping us in my poofy cloud of curls.
     He loves my hair the most.
Now he grabs my face in both his hands and
kisses my forehead—

Every day since we started dating, he's had to
remind me that he doesn't care how bad my skin
looks, that I'm still beautiful, and he always
runs his hand over my lion's mane.
That's what he calls it: my lion's mane.

And to think I used to want it straight and blond
like Kate's. But Micah says it's   *exotic*—
My Black mixed with white.
My mermaid mixed with white.

My invisibility mixed with, "What are you?"

"I'm biracial," I've been saying my whole life.
Except the Black part of me might as well be a
dream—an unknown thing in the shape of an
absent mother that haunts me at night.

And now Micah grazes my cheek with the
back of his hand and it doesn't hurt—

"So Kate got a nanny for the twins," I say
as we walk down to Flatbush Avenue. I talk to
Micah about basic shit. Not about my
nightmares, not about how bad my skin gets,
and definitely not about this weird feeling
I have about that new lady in our house.
"And she had this . . . I don't know.
She had this remedy or oil or something.
        And it worked!"

I don't believe my own words because
there was nothing in Lourdes's hands.
Or maybe I just didn't see it.
But it worked—   For now.

 V

Dad hates Micah.

When I first realized this, I called him a
        racist—
Dad hates this neighborhood.
Whenever he steps off our (historic landmark) block,
he complains about the trash, the noise, the people,
so I call him a
        racist—
Dad hates my school.
When I decided to leave my almost all-white private
school to apply for a public performing arts high school
and he tried to talk me out of it, I called him a
        racist—

"Gen, I can't have an opinion without being called a
        racist?" he'd asked one day.
"I mean, look around. Does it look like a racist lives here?"

It's true. With all the African and Caribbean art we have
around the house, it's clear that Dad loves Black culture.
But when Micah first came over, he said, "It's like the
        British Museum up in here."

This was one of the few times that Kate had my back,
and she said, "I get it, Gen. You want to be around kids
        who look like you."

So I go to Brooklyn Performing Arts Academy in Flatbush,

which is a few blocks from my house. Except
the school shares this giant building with other schools
in what used to be Erasmus Hall High. Its claim to fame
is that some lady named Barbra Streisand is an alumni.
But over the years, it got a bad reputation, so
they divided it up into five schools on four floors.

And each school is   a different world—
Like, I swear I have to walk through a battlefield
just to get to the fourth floor where BPAA is. Micah goes
to one of the other schools. I met him while walking home.
So we're like in two different worlds in the same building.

He lives in Flatbush. I live in Prospect Lefferts Gardens.
Two different worlds in the same neighborhood.

        He is the entire Caribbean all in one soul.
I am a cultural artifact in a museum in a landmark home
        in the middle of the hood.
Two different worlds—

So we hold hands when we walk down the busy street.
Together, we're Brooklyn in all its contradictions—

But today,   I make sense.
All the jagged pieces of me have come together
because everyone sees me.   Like, the real me

under all that inflamed   skin—
And they say   hi
like they always do.   But today, I must be the sun—

"Hey, Gen!"   "What up, Gen!"
    "Hi, Genevieve!"

Micah has always been popular.
Point guard on his school's basketball team.
And I guess I'm popular too because—

"You look different," Micah always says.

And the other girls remind me of that too.
"The basketball players want the light-skinned girls,"
Rena and Trish always say. So Rena dates a baller too.
But not Trish.   Micah says he just has a preference.
So if I'm his preference, I can't fault him for that.

Being mixed is better than being a straight-up white girl.
    Especially at this school—

So I hold Micah's arm because today
I am more than some mixed chick with good hair;
    more than some pretty girl with bad skin—

Today, I am   the sun and   the sky.

VI

"Move, you ugly bitch!" Micah says to someone
    as I hold his arm.

Then some girl trips and falls right next to us.

Rena and Trish are a few feet ahead of me and they
turn around. Trish says, "You outta pocket for that,
Micah," and she starts laughing—
So Micah starts laughing too,
but I tug his arm for him to stop—

I hate when he gets mean like this.

I look at the girl who stays on the ground
never getting up, never dusting herself off,
and never picking up her pride—

And everyone keeps laughing
and   laughing   and   laughing—

I walk around her like everyone else does because
it's just another day at this school—
Just another day of some kid getting cursed out—
Just another day of a fight, a threat, a suspension,
an expulsion, and chaos—
I've had to get thick skin just to be here,
        literally.

Micah puts his arm around my shoulders
and we walk up the steps and through the doors.

"You look so pretty today," he says, and kisses me
before a security guard forces us apart
because we go to different schools.
        We belong to different worlds—

And everything today will be soft clouds and sunshine.
And I will dance like   the universe is watching.
And there's no pain. No heat on my skin. Just a calming
coolness   settling in my core—

—MARISOL

Home

I did not see his face. I do not know his name.
But I have the memory of the sound of his
laughter—
I have the memory of the sound of his
voice calling me
ugly—

On the islands, we are much more poetic
with our insults. Callous words are wrapped
in metaphor. Profanity is sprinkled with sugar
so the words are not so sharp; so the wounds are
not so deep.

Here, words are machete blades.
They don't slice or cut. They chop.
They mutilate.　　　　They grind
into dust.

No one helped me get up from the ground.
I stayed there because I was waiting for my
wings to sprout.
I was waiting for my skin to shed
and my firesoul to ignite
right then and there.

But today I am just a girl
wearing the skin they gave me:

Black   poor   immigrant

ugly—

Where is Mummy? Where is my mother
to remind me of the skin she gave me,
the one that tells the world that

I   am   incomprehensible?

That I am so powerful and cosmic,
no words, no insults, and not even
a compliment can explain all that I am.

II

So I look for her in all the store windows
on Flatbush Avenue—the fruit-and-vegetable
markets; the clothing stores and restaurants
whose gates are still down; and even up at the
apartment windows in case she is in a
stranger's home cleaning their mess.

I stop in front of a fast-food place.
We have them on the islands.
We protested them on the islands.
We did not want any foreigners

taking up more space, more land
on our home. But they came with
their burgers and French fries,
fried chicken and pizza.

And we island people did not
realize how hungry we were
for the world—

It is still breakfast time.
So I order a bacon, egg, and cheese
bagel with orange juice and
dig into my jeans pocket
for the cash I took
from the bakery.

Money earned and money owed.

And this morning, with my jaw
still in pain, with my pride
still in pain, I eat like
I have never eaten
before—

And fill my belly up with
this fast American food.
Not a healing balm for my hurt soul.

Not a nourishing meal for my bruised body.
But a   Band-Aid
for a slow-healing wound—

I walk back down to the bakery
and pass all the store windows
reflecting back to me the skin
I am wearing, the clothes
I am wearing, the face
I am wearing.

My chin, my head, my body hurts.

III

The sign on the bakery's door now says *Open*.
Jaden is already serving a customer at the
register. He sees me and he points up.

I don't know what he is saying.
Then he furrows his brow and touches his chin.
So I touch my chin too, and it's wet. Blood.
Where is my mother?

The customer leaves and Jaden rushes to me.
"What happened to your face?" he asks.

"The kids here are the monsters," I say.
"Not me."

He gently takes my face in his hands
and licks   my chin. Tastes my blood.
I let him. And my insides simmer again.
But I am too angry to melt in his arms.
I will   burn him   if I don't get away.

"Go upstairs quick!"
he says, stepping back,
and one of the workers comes in
and runs into the kitchen.

"What is going on?" I ask.

"Jean-Pierre's wife is back and she called
everyone to return to work. She asked
for you and your mother."

I don't even wait for Jaden to explain
further, and I rush upstairs to see our
apartment door wide open.

Jean-Pierre's wife is standing in front
of the broken window—

She has always been kind to us,
so I say, "I can explain."

But her face is different now.
She glares at me as if   as if
she has seen a   monster—

She points to the mortar in the corner.

"I can explain," I repeat.

"Where is Lourdes?" she asks.
Her voice is like a thin thread
ready to snap at any moment.
"Where is   Lourdes?"

"She   she   went to find work.
She has not been paid. . . ."

"Lougarou," Jean-Pierre's wife
whispers under her breath.
"I know what she did to my husband."

I clench my fists because I know this song.
I know this melody. I know this story.

"We are not on the islands anymore,
Madame Jean-Pierre," I say.
"You cannot make these accusations."

She keeps pointing to the mortar.
It is true. Anyone who sees it and
believes in our old stories will know
what we are.
But there is always an explanation.
There is always room for doubt.

"Madame Jean-Pierre, you know my mother
is a woman of God," I say, stepping
closer to her so that she knows
I am safe.   I am human.
For now.

"Get away from me!" she shouts.
"Look what you did to this place!
Look what your mother did
to my husband!"

I won't tell her that it was me.
I will let her blame my mother.
This was Mummy's battle and not mine.

Rage doesn't trigger
our shifting. Only the moon.
At times like this,
I wish we could call on our
monstrosity for protection—
but we are always at the
mercy of   nature.

"You have to leave," she hisses.
"Get out of our building!
You and your mother cannot
live or work here anymore."

Footsteps are coming up the stairs.
My insides are stirring with heat.
But I can't do anything
except stand here and—

"Madame Jean-Pierre," my mother's
voice says from behind me.

V

Mummy is wearing the same dress she left in.
But something is different about her.
She looks as if she found what
she was looking for, and maybe
it is money. More money.

"Take your garbage and leave!"

Madame Jean-Pierre shouts.
She is backing away from us.
Scared of us. As if we will
attack her right then and there.

But we are in the flesh
just like her.
We are just a girl and her mother
who need a place to live;
who need a   home.

"We do not want any trouble," Mummy says.
"We need some time to gather our things."
She glances over at the mortar.

Madame Jean-Pierre narrows her eyes at my mother,
then she goes over to the mortar and kicks it.
It drops to the floor with a hard thud,
and it rolls to Mummy's feet as if for protection.

"Don't touch my things!" Mummy shouts.

I clench my fists even tighter.
We will not hurt her. But we will
remember her one month from now
when it's time for   vengeance—

Mummy and Madame Jean-Pierre
lock eyes as if one wrong move
will start a war.

"Leave this place!"
Madame Jean-Pierre shouts again.
"And I hope you burn in hell
for what you did to my husband!"

She backs away, stepping out of the
apartment without ever turning her back to us;
without ever looking away from us.

Maybe she already knows
that hell is here in this new country.
Every day, someone is made into a
monster.

VI

"We have to hurry!" Mummy says
as she rushes to the mortar. "Grab your things.
Take only what you need."

"Where will we go now?" I ask,
dumping my clothes into my suitcase.

"We will live where I work," she says.

"Again?" I ask.
"Mummy, we should separate work from life
so this does not happen again. I am tired of
running." I stop and look at her,
waiting for an answer; waiting for a
change in direction—

"This time will be different, Marisol.
I am taking care of babies,"
she says, stopping to look over at me
with a big, bright smile—
Then her smile disappears.
"What happened to your face?"

"I fell," I say, and quickly change the subject.
"Babies? Mummy, you will be taking care
of *babies*? Then we are going to
be running again. If anything happens to
the babies, they will blame us like
they always do."

"The people I work for do not
believe these stories are true. Well, one of
them doesn't." She comes over to me and
reaches for my chin. I let her touch where
it is sore, where there is blood.
The familiar coolness of her hand
travels to every part of my skin.

Then the cold—
Then the healing—
This is Mummy's magic too.

We can destroy
and we can heal.
But I am still learning how
to perfect my cooling touch.

"Mummy, you should help Jean-Pierre heal faster.
Word is getting around that we are
what they say we are," I tell my mother,
because she is not thinking this through.
"We can't keep moving around like this.
I thought it would be different here."

She doesn't respond and only
touches the rest of my face,
searching for any more
bruises or blemishes.

"A home, Mari. A beautiful home!"
is all she says and takes both my hands.
Her eyes are watering as if she has found
true happiness in this home. "Our home."

I smile a little too, because in her voice
is a sliver of light, a sliver of hope.

If Mummy says we have a home,
I will follow that sliver of light
to the edge of the sky.

But *babies*?
We will have to be very careful.
I will have to be very careful.

So again, we leave. So again, we run.
But this time,
there are no borders to cross;
there are no forests to conquer;
there is no ocean to bargain with;
there is no sky to traverse.

There is a car outside waiting for us
as we leave with our two suitcases
and the giant mortar—

I turn back to Jaden in the bakery
and I don't smile. I give him nothing.
He waves and grins. He will know
to find me in the sky on the
night of a new moon.

Madame Jean-Pierre is in the bakery window
with her eyes glaring, scowling. Fearful.
I mouth, "I am sorry."

I don't like when people think the worst of us.

In the car, a white man is driving
and I realize quickly that this is not
a taxicab. Mummy sits in the passenger
seat, and I have more questions
than she can answer right now.
The man quickly turns to me from the
driver's seat and says,
"You must be Marisol."

I just stare at him because this is   new.
"Where are we going again, Mummy?" I ask, to make
sure that my life will be the life I dreamed of—

Mummy turns back to me, smiling wide
and says, "I already told you. We are going home."

The man sighs as if this is a discussion they have
already had, and I'm not sure he has agreed to this.
"I'm Daniel," he says, smiling nervously.

"Home?" I ask one last time.

"Yes," my mother says. "Home."

GENEVIEVE—

Home

I'm the most at home
in dance class, in my own
skin   whenever it's calm
and normal like this.

When I dance, heat begs to break
     through my body—
An imaginary thread pulls each part
of my limbs towards every corner of the space,

and   I feel like
     I can tear down walls if I want to.
     I can fly towards the moon
         and become the universe if I want to.
     I can dive into the deepest waters
         and become the ocean if I want to.

I can dance out of my skin if I want to—

But my classmates, my friends, my teacher,
this school   ·   always hold me back.

"This is not a solo, Genevieve," the teacher says.

"Why she think she always gotta outshine everybody?"
I hear Rena say to Trish.

But Micah is my biggest fan.
"Did you hear back from that school yet?" he asks
after my last class, and I've already changed out
of my dance clothes. Ever since we started
dating at the end of junior year, I spend more
time with him than with Rena and Trish.

"It's not just *that* school, Micah.
It's *the* Juilliard School.   And no.
Acceptance letters go out in the spring."

He takes my bags and carries them
down the stairs, like he always does.
A gentleman—   But no one believes
me when I tell them that he treats me like
a queen when he treats everyone else like shit.

"No flare-ups today?" he asks,
because he always notices the red patches
after I dance and sweat;
how I wince when he touches me.

"No," I say, remembering the woman who
is waiting for me back home—

II

Micah walks me down Flatbush Avenue.
    We always hold hands.

He always makes sure no guys stare
at me. He always makes sure that I'm safe.

We pass a spot called Island Bakery and we
usually avoid it because of my gluten allergy,
    but today, maybe I can let it slide.
I remember the breakfast the nanny had made.
I remember how I didn't
    have a reaction to anything I'd eaten.
I remember how that island food soothed my
soul, and maybe today I can celebrate
not being   in pain;
not feeling like   my skin is on fire.

"Can you get me some fried bake?" I ask Micah.

"I got something even better:
beef patty and coco bread," he says, smiling.

We walk in together, and a dark-skinned
boy is at the register staring at me.
Just staring at me—

"The fuck you looking at?" Micah says.
My whole body tenses up because

I hate when he gets like this.

"Oh, I'm sorry, is that your girlfriend?"
the boy responds with a smirk.

"What'd you say?" Micah stares him down
                    as if he's ready to deck him.

"Chill, Micah!" I pull his arm, forcing
him to step back and calm down.
"Don't do this here, please."

He calls it chivalry.

I call it embarrassing.

"Gen, he's toxic," Trish had told me once.

And I made the mistake of telling Micah.

And he just said, "Can't you see she's jealous
of you? She's not a baddie like you. . . ."

So my boyfriend defends me,
even though he's playing offense—

like I'm a three-point shot;
    a Division I scholarship;
        a trophy.

Micah calms down, but he still clenches his
fists and tightens his jaw as if that boy
wants to fight him for me.

A black cat leaps from behind the counter and lands
right next to Micah's leg, startling both of us.
Micah kicks it and it meows, scurrying away.

"Really, Micah! What'd that cat do to you?"
I ask, completely pissed at him now. Then I
say to the boy, "Can I get a beef patty and
coco bread?" I smile to de-escalate the situation.

"We don't have any," the boy says.

Micah sighs and throws his head back.
"My mom *been* complaining about this place.
Y'all used to have everything, but now . . ."

But before he gets heated again,
I say, "I'll take whatever you have."

The boy places a loaf of plain bread
in a brown paper bag—its crust is smooth

and as soon as he hands it to me, I break
off a piece and the inside is soft like clouds.
I take a mouthful—
My skin is better now. I should be able to
eat what I want—

"This is some bullshit," Micah says.
"My mom heard something happened to the owner.
And now they're selling old bread.
Don't pay for that shit."

"I got it," I mumble, digging for my wallet.

But Micah grabs my hand—

I'm about to pull away so that I can put a few
dollars into the tip jar, but I spot a photo
of a woman taped to the door with the word
LOUGAROU scribbled across
                    her face in big red letters.

I stop and ask the boy, "What's this?"

"Nothing," he says, staring at me again.

Micah tugs my arm to leave, and I take another
good look at the woman in the photo. It's blurry,
but the picture was taken right here in this bakery

behind the cash register where the boy is.
I blink and blink and blink to make sure
that what I'm seeing is what I'm seeing—

Lourdes.

I want to tear the photo from off the door,
but Micah pulls me out and we rush down
Flatbush to my block and I'm holding the brown
paper bag with the bread that I didn't pay for.

I don't take another bite, thinking of that word:
    lougarou.
Thinking of that woman:
    Lourdes.

"You know what a lougarou is?"
I ask Micah as we turn down my block.

He kisses his teeth and says,
"Yeah. Lougarou in Haiti. Soucouyant in Trinidad.
Old hag in Jamaica. Same shit, different island.
My mother believes in those stories. Her church
friends are always accusing somebody of being a
witch or a shape-shifter or whatever—
It's superstition. Like ghosts, vampires,
zombies and all that . . ."
I don't ask him anything else because

while Micah was raised with these stories
as part of his culture, I was raised with
these stories as part of my life.
While he thinks they're just superstition,
my father believes they're science.

And that bakery is accusing Lourdes
of being one of them—
It had to be her.

And she's living in my house right now.

"You good?" Micah asks before we reach
my brownstone. "Is it okay if I come over?"

I want to tell him not to come to my house.
I want to talk to him and ask him big questions
about nightmares and myth, intuition and superstition.
But I don't want him to think I'm weird.
      I don't want him to clown me the way
he clowns everybody else.
      He can be such an asshole sometimes.

But we're already here, standing on the steps,
when Lourdes opens the door for us.

III

"Welcome back home, Genevieve," she says
with that singsong voice of hers.
My name rolls off her tongue like a spell.

We walk past her, avoiding her, and I wonder
if Micah recognizes her from the photo in the bakery.

In the parlor room, a girl is holding one of the babies.
She cradles Elliott   as if he's a fragile little thing
     that will break   in her arms—

I rush over to take him from her, but I can't stop
     staring at   her face—

     How her deep-set eyes stare back at mine—
     How her full lips are slightly open—
     How her round nose and full cheeks
          are so   familiar—

"Oh, this is my, eh . . . ," Lourdes starts,
gently pulling me away from this girl.
"This is my . . . daughter,   Marisol."

I   can't   stop   staring   at her.

"Marisol, this is my . . .   This is Genevieve,"
Lourdes continues.

She finally takes baby Elliott from the girl,
        Marisol—

And in that moment, a tingling sensation
rises from the soles of my feet to reach
all the way up to the top of my head. My face burns
and I touch my skin to feel the bumps slowly, slowly raising—

It's starting again.

The allergy. The eczema.
Whatever it is, it's coming back—
I'm suddenly feeling as if
        my skin will burn and melt
            right off my fucking bones.

And that girl   that girl
        keeps staring at me   staring at me
            and I swear

        she has my face—
        she has the smooth skin I want—
        she is me   but   like
            a nighttime version of me—

                        "Hello, Genevieve,"
she says, pronouncing my name the French way.

And I swear, my name rolls off her tongue like a spell.

                                        "And you are ?"
she asks.

And it's not until when Micah comes from
behind me that I finally stop staring.

"How you doing? I'm Micah," he says.

                                        "Oh. Micah,"
she repeats,
with the same accent as Lourdes's.

And I look   over at   Lourdes
who is looking   at me   and this girl
like she is watching
                    a rare total eclipse—

TWO

FATHER SUN

—MARISOL

Family

Mummy took me to work with her
for the first time when
I was six years old.
This was when I understood
what it meant to   hide.

She snuck me in through the back
doors at the resorts. I curled my little body
among dirty linens in the laundry rooms.
I hid beneath carts and tables in
large kitchens and restaurants.
I sat in the shade and made myself
a shadow of a girl beneath
palm trees and beach umbrellas
along the white sandy shores.

And in a few years' time,
I traded in my secondhand
T-shirts for my own uniform.
Girls like me start working at the resorts
as early as age twelve.

The same time we start to shift and fly.

I was never alone—

the other women brought their children too.
The boys helped with the luggage and groundskeeping.
Us girls weaved in and out of the tourists like
hummingbirds, except at night when we became
what we really are—each of us a different folklore
come to life at dusk, at midnight, or at dawn.

When we did not have our own mortars,
we watched over our sisters' skins.
When the scientists and scholars from
all over the world came to steal our stories;
came to expose our magic,   we banded
together to divert their attention   or,

we hunted them in the night—

Back home,   all the magical beings
were my family—
            Here, we divide ourselves so that we
are   not   conquered.

We can never know who is family,
and who is enemy;
            who is monster and who is prey,

                  until night comes;
                  until the new moon—

II

In this house that is not my home,
I watch my mother dust every corner,
cook every meal, clean every soiled thing
and become the mother I never knew—

In this house that is not my home
is proof that we exist—
Our stories are written in leather-bound
books and I swear the pages are made
from our skins—

In this house that is not my home
is a man who believes that our magic
is real and that he can study it
like cells under a microscope and
maybe he hides some of us
in a secret lab to poke   and prod
our bodies looking for
the   truth; looking for
the   god in us.

In this house that is not my home
is a collection of wooden mortars
and the collector's name is Daniel—
a doctor of philosophy
in anthropology
at some big university—

People like him come to our resorts
with their conferences and lectures,
trying to explain to each other our magic
and make it into a   science.

"Those men there," Mummy had told me once,
"they like to destroy things in order to
understand them. They do not know
that magic belongs to the soul
and not the mind."

Daniel is too stupid to know
that we are   incomprehensible.

But still, what does he already know about us?
Why does Mummy call this place our home when
they are not family; they are not even magical kin?

III

In this house that is not my home
are three babies. Two are brand-new
and the other is two years older than me.

Her name is Genevieve—

and my mother cares for her
like she is a princess.

Genevieve flutters around the house
like a butterfly, leaving clothes
and towels everywhere; picking at
her food; complaining about the heat,
the cold, her hair, her face,
her skin—

Her skin
with its rashes, blemishes,
and inflammations,

looks like mine when I was twelve,
except   much lighter;
looks like all the young soucouyant
and lougarou who are slowly,
slowly coming into their magic,
except   much lighter.

But   Genevieve is seventeen.
Genevieve is not from the islands.
Genevieve lives with her white father
and a white mother who is not
her mother—

And this is a deep forest
of a mystery I am not willing to walk into.
Not yet. She is not my enemy   yet.

Genevieve has a face I have come
to know so well—

How her eyes can pierce into a soul—
How her thick lips turn down when
she is sad—
How her smile is like the new moon,
full of secrets, full of unseen and unknown
magic—

When Genevieve stands next to my mother
and my eyes move from one face to another,
questions, answers, secrets, and lies
become a cosmic storm in my mind—
a collision of galaxies,
crashing into each other
to expose   one   big truth.

What is this place?
Who are these people?
Who is that girl?

What is this family   to us?

IV

Kate asks me too many questions.
She is so distracted by her own

life that she does not see that
the answers are under her nose.

"You are so beautiful," she tells me,
looking at my skin and not my eyes,
where beauty is supposed to live.
"You have to share your skin-care
routine with Gen."

"Really, Kate?"

Gen says as she comes into the kitchen
where we all gather with the babies.

"You really went there, huh?"

Genevieve always looks as if she
wants to fight this woman
who is not her mother.
And Kate ignores her, as if this is a
daily dance between them,
a daily fight between them.

"And Marisol is such a unique name.
Where do you go to school, Marisol?"
Kate says, but I know that
she does not really care.

I am just   extra help—
An extra pair of hands for the twins.
An extra body in this cold museum of a house.

"Her school is close to here," Mummy answers
for me as she sets the table for breakfast.
"On Flatbush Avenue. I will have to
give them my new home address."

"Oh, she goes to Gen's school!"
Kate says, glancing over at her
daughter who is not her daughter.
"I mean, the building houses
many schools, but you must go to the one
that takes anybody. So you'll probably need
proof of residence, which I can give you. . . ."

Mummy sounds as if she's
inhaling a serpent
and I know that feeling—
I become worried for Kate.
At least she'll have someone
to take care of her babies if
she suddenly becomes
sick—

So Mama changes the subject
by offering Genevieve
breakfast before she rushes out the door.
"Cornmeal porridge is good for you
on this cold morning," she says,
setting a place mat for her,
and sometimes I think

Mummy forgets that I am here.

Genevieve never refuses
my mother's food.
I watch her as she contemplates
a piece of bread.
Her face looks bad this morning—
blotchy, red, painful maybe.
Her hands are covered in rashes
and Mummy would know what to do,
but part of me does not want
my mother to help this girl.
I'm not sure I like her either.

But I'm sure she doesn't
want me in her space like this.
She doesn't speak to me.
But she stares at me as if I'm
a ghost living in her house.

Genevieve takes a bite of the bread
slowly, cautiously, as if she thinks
my mother is trying to poison her.

V

Two more weeks until the
new moon—
Two more weeks until me and Mummy have
to shift and fly—
Two more weeks until we have to seek
sustenance—

And I remember the sound of his voice
saying   *ugly*—
I remember the sound of his laughter—

It was him. It was this boy
who called me ugly and made me fall.

I hear the boy named Micah
tell his girlfriend that she is beautiful;
tell his girlfriend that she is a "baddie";
tell his girlfriend that they are going to be
together forever—

I listen to them.

I watch them
as Genevieve sneaks him up to her
bedroom where there is nothing but
the sound of   secrets.

VI

Mummy and I share a cloud-soft bed
like the ones at the resorts.
And we have our own bathroom too.
Both rooms are large enough
for each of us to have our own
thoughts and dreams.

But this entire house is not large
enough for us to have our own
magic—

We don't have the privacy we need.
The owners of this house
live, eat, and sleep right below us.

"Mummy," I carefully say as we settle
in for the night, even though I know
she will be up again when
the babies start to cry.
"Where will we hide this time?"

She clicks her tongue at me—
"Ah, Mari. What did I tell you?" she says,
annoyed. "We are home.
There is no need to hide."

And in that moment, heat stirs in my belly.
Not heat from the flame that burns
within my soucouyant soul.
This heat is from the gut feeling that
Mummy's secrets are much deeper
than I can ever imagine.

Who has hurt her?
Who will she name?
What will she ask of me?
And who will have
a sudden bout
of fever and illness

after the next time
we shift and fly and
settle back into
our skins

to make this house
into a home?

Love

Today is Daniel's birthday
and Kate has asked my mother
to make a surprise Caribbean meal.

But Daniel is hardly home,
and when he is, he pours
all his time into the babies—
Genevieve is hardly home,
and when she is, she pours
all her time into her phone, talking
to the boy named Micah—

I hear Kate complaining to my mother.
"I mean, where am I in all of this?"
she says over coffee, and Mummy
is discouraging her from having a
glass of wine while she is still nursing.
"Not only do I have to find my old self
in this new role, I have to make sure
my husband of sixteen years
still finds me attractive!"
Her blond hair is pulled up into
a loose bun. She wears exercise clothes
even though I have not seen her exercise.

"You are beautiful, Ms. Kate,"
Mummy says. "In time, your
new mothering self will emerge
out of your old self, and she will
be even more beautiful."

Kate is like the tourists at the resorts
who sit at the bars with their cocktails
and problems hoping that the workers
will save them from their lives.

And at some point, they turn their
attention to us as if this is a game
of whose life is more miserable.
So Kate says, "Enough about me.
What about you, Lourdes?
Was there someone special in your life?
Did you leave them behind?"

They are in the kitchen and I am on the couch
watching the babies as they sleep in their bassinets.
This house has no walls.
Kate calls it *open concept*.
So I press my ear against the gaping space,
waiting to hear what Mummy will say about
someone special in her life; waiting to hear
her say my father's name   for the first time.

But Mummy laughs (a rare sound) and says,
"Oh no. I am much too busy raising my daughter."

This is true. And I don't know my father—

"Well, your daughter had to come from somewhere!"
Kate says, sipping from her coffee mug.
"Where is he? What's his name?"

I glance at Mummy, who is gathering her ingredients
for tonight's dinner and placing them on the counter.
She hides her eyes when she doesn't want
anyone to see her feelings—
Her hair is wrapped in a blue scarf
and Kate has not offered her a new uniform,
new clothes, anything to let her know that
this is a real job—

How is this our home, anyway?

"Aww, come on, Lourdes!" Kate sings.
"Island love stories are the best!
I should know. Daniel and I got married
at this place called the Hibiscus.

You used to work there, right?

I recognized that uniform dress
from the first day I saw it on you."

I look directly at Mummy, and our eyes meet.

She quickly turns away and says,
"Oh, this dress is from . . . a friend.
I did not work there."

That is a lie. We have only worked at all
the Hibiscus Resort locations—

"Well, Daniel loves that place.
He first went when he was in college.
We were only dating then.
He kept going back. . . ." Kate's voice gets
softer and much farther away, as if she is
lost in some old memory—
"I mean, it was like he was always
leaving something behind. . . ."

"Ms. Kate, I think it is time to feed the
twins!" Mummy interrupts, rushing to
pick up one of the babies, who
is still asleep.

"My first time there, he proposed,"
Kate continues.

"Down on one knee with a
cheap ring and all.
And then it was his idea to have a
destination wedding. I wanted
somewhere else, another
island all together. Or even Florida.
I thought, *What is it about that place?*
He couldn't get enough of the Caribbean.
I mean, I loved that resort, too, until . . ."

The babies start to cry.

And I am still holding on to Kate's
words as if they are keys on a ring.

One more detail—
just one more detail will unlock
a door I did not even know was there.

II

I have always seen my mother cook.
She has cooked for the restaurants
at the resorts. She has cooked for
both strangers and friends.
And she has cooked for me—

meals with recipes that are carved into our daily lives.
Meals that have been prepared over open flames
to remind us that this is the sacred sustenance
for our bodies, but not for our soucouyant souls.

But for this meal, she seems to be pouring
her actual entire soul into every dish—

Daniel's presence in this house is as if
he is a visitor in his own home,
only stepping in to see his children.
Kate tries to kiss him when he arrives,
but he pulls away every time—

Mummy moves around Daniel as if he
is some awkwardly placed furniture
she is trying to avoid—
but he moves around my mother as if
she is something   forbidden.

And I know this song.
I know this rhythm.

Tourists always want to taste all our
island flavors,   including us—
If Daniel loves the Caribbean that much,
maybe he wants my mother to work here forever,

to cook island meals for him and his family
until the end of time—

But how is this place home
where she still has to work?
How is this the American dream?

At the resorts, the tourists who know our stories
and believe in our magic will end up accusing us
of something and anything. They think we are
monsters and only monsters. A missing child,
a sudden illness, a seduced husband—
they will point their fingers and call us
what we are: soucouyant, lougarou, old hag.

Nightmares.

So we run, bouncing from job to job,
island to island, resort to resort, home to home.
And in this house that is not my home,
I leave my bags packed.

III

Kate goes upstairs to change. She takes the girl baby
with her. Mummy stays with the boy baby. I stay.
Daniel stays. Why doesn't Mummy let me hide in the

room the same way I hid at the bakery?
Here, I always have to   help.

So I move to the front of the house
to be invisible. There is a fireplace mantel where
Daniel keeps his collection of small mortars,
and he knows about soucouyant. He knows
about lougarou. There are books all over
the house about our magic—Caribbean folktales,
African mythology, carnival characters, vodou spirits.

He knows   something.
But he can never know   everything.

And voices echo in from the kitchen.
Daniel   is whispering, but it's still
loud enough for me to hear—
I tiptoe closer and make myself
like an insect on a wall—

"I don't know how long I can keep up
with these charades, Lourdes,"
Daniel whispers. "Something's gotta give."

"Please, let me help her first.
Then you can tell her the truth,"
Mummy says softly.

And I swallow a big gulp of air.
She hears me—

"Marisol?" she says.

And I hold my breath—

The front door opens.
Genevieve walks in—

She sees me leaning
against a bookshelf
near the kitchen.

Daniel walks out.
He extends his arms
to give his daughter a hug.

But Genevieve is looking at me,
just looking at me—

"Happy Birthday, Dad,"

she says, with sadness in her voice.

Her father hugs her.   She hisses.
"It hurts. Everything hurts,"

she says with a small voice.

Mummy walks out with the baby and
looks at me, just looks at me—
I try to speak with my eyes.
I blink as if to ask,
What is going on, Mummy?

Genevieve rushes to my mother
and says,

"Do that thing you did
the other day. You put something on
my skin and made it better.
What was that?"

Her face is red.
It looks like her skin   is on fire.

I step closer to get a better look.

And the moon,   sun,   and stars
collide into one big possibility—

Is Genevieve   one of us?

But I don't dare say those words out loud.

"Let us go upstairs," Mummy says softly.

At the same time, Kate calls her name
because the girl baby starts crying.
So the boy baby starts crying too—

And Daniel is standing there,
just standing there,
and I am right next to
him in the middle of this
BIG BANG of
confusion.

"Who   are   you?"
I finally ask the collector—

I did not expect him to say a word.
I did not expect him to answer.

"Twenty years ago today," he starts,
looking down and biting his lip.
His eyes are green, his hair is
light brown, his skin is pale.
"I fell in love with   your mother."

And the air   the air
in this house   in this house
grows hot   hot

                                         and I want to
                implode   implode
                right then and there,
                but I can't.   I can't let rage
                loose   on everyone   in this house
                                                  that is not my home—
                                                          not yet.

                                    We both didn't know that
                Genevieve   had been standing there,
                just standing there at the top of the stairs
                          when her father excavates this truth—

                          He digs it from the pit of my mother
                                         like buried gold,
                                         and holds it up for us to see
                as if   this truth   is the sun—

                And I know,   I know
                          that Daniel is more than a collector—
                                    He is a pillager and
                                    my mother is the scorched earth.

                                         Did she even want
                                    this truth to come out like this?

She comes down and stares at him,
just stares at him as if she wants
to   implode too—
As if   she wants to let rage
loose on everyone in this house
that is her home—

Soon.   Soon, maybe.

GENEVIEVE—

Family

I take her hand and put it on my forehead.
I force her to do that thing she did the other
morning. "Make it stop," I say through
clenched teeth, through the pain, through the
burning—

But nothing changes.
I look at her. I look into her eyes.
I look at her deep brown, smooth skin—
I touch her cheek.
She takes my hand and holds it there like
I can do   magic too—

I had pulled her into my bedroom,
even as Kate was calling her name
and the twins were crying in their nursery.

I leave Dad downstairs with that girl.
I leave that girl downstairs with my dad.

I take this woman that my father
fell in love with into my room and
demand the truth; demand her magic—

They owe me this moment.
This nanny, this woman, this mermaid (maybe)
owes me this moment.

"Are you a   mermaid?" I ask.
Because I need my father's folktales
to make sense of reality right now.
I need to know if my origin story is true.

"No," she says quietly, with tears glistening
in her eyes. "I have never been a mermaid."

"Are you a   lougarou then?"
     I ask her straight up.
"The photo of you at the bakery says so."

That way she can't lie to me. No one can lie to me.
I want the truth   wrapped in folklore;
wrapped in   magic and myth—
I step back away from her because
                    monsters are real—
Maybe I   came from one.

She eases closer to me, even as I tense up, and
I don't know what a mother monster
                    will do to her own—
But I let her take both my hands in hers and she
turns them over. My skin has been feeling like hell

these past couple of days and I was afraid to ask her for
help—
But today my skin was an inferno. I didn't want to show
my face at school. I kept dodging Micah. Even my
fiery dancing was not enough to
melt my skin away—
And I wanted so badly to rise out of my own
dissolved body like a phoenix out of ashes.

"I tried to tell you. I tried to visit you in your dreams.
I tried to show you what you are. But I could not find
you, until now. I found you. I found you!" Lourdes says
through soft sobs and
my heart shatters into a billion pieces.

Is this what truth feels like?
An earthquake in my soul?
A fault line on my skin?

She leaves me, goes upstairs to her room,
and comes back with a jar of something smelly.
I dreamed this. I wished this. I knew this was real.

"This is not magic," she says. "This is just coconut oil.
I am still searching for the herbs we had on the islands.
A balm for the skin,   but not for the soul—
I cannot stop what is bound to happen. Not so close
to the new moon."

She sits me down at the edge of my bed
and scoops out a dollop of the coconut oil
and gently spreads it across the top of my hands.
It's soothing, but she's right. It's not magic.

"I was able to ease the burning a few days ago,"
she continues,
"but now,   it is almost time. I cannot stop it."

"Time   for what?" I ask.
I know what she's talking about.
The new moon is always time for
magic, for change, for shifting.
But I need her to spell it out for me.
I need her to just say it!

But Kate calls both our names and
I wish she would just leave us alone—

"Where've you been all this time?" I ask,
my voice shaking. I blink back tears.

She looks down. Guilt maybe.
She inhales. Truth maybe. Finally.
She pulls me in for a hug like I'm some
lost thing that's been found. Finally found.

And I become a storm—

a torrent of   rage, guilt, confusion, and
          relief.

And I sob   and sob and sob and
I wrap my arms around her warm body
          not wanting to ever, ever let go.

And it doesn't hurt. It doesn't burn.

I never thought that she
would be made of fire
and not the ocean—

I never thought that she
would be the monster in the stories
my father told me—

But I am not afraid of this monster
that made me—

Her name is Lourdes.   Lourdes.

II

And I'm pissed at my father—

Lourdes and I agree to get through this
dinner as if everything is normal.

But I have questions.
I need new stories.
I need my father to turn the page of this
storybook called my life to where the
magic begins—

And for my father's birthday,
Lourdes sets the table as if
this is a holiday—

"We have jerk chicken, rice and peas,
callaloo, ground provisions . . . ,"
she sings with a wide smile and
I can't stop looking at her face—
Her face that has always been the moon;
her face that has always been the ocean;
her face that has always been the flames.

How are we supposed to go on as
if my life has not just imploded?
Did she come back for me?
Was Dad hiding her from me this whole time?

"Smells delish!" Kate says, and she
doesn't even know what's going on.
This will break her heart too.
So I agree to keep my mouth shut just to

protect her; just to protect Bethany and Elliott.

I'm still trying to wrap my entire universe around
what this all means. My father's books are supposed
to have answers. His research papers have made
science out of magic. His lectures try to prove
that there's a whole other world where humans,
magic, and the cosmos can exist in one soul.

And I wonder if he fell in love with Lourdes,
        or   his research—

Part of me wants to grab as many of my father's
books as I can to read up on what Lourdes is—
a lougarou, a soucouyant, a shape-shifting
soul-sucking flying meteor witch.

Some books have pictures. Some books
only have words to describe what she is.
But I need to see it,
I need to feel it   to know that it's real;
that she's real;   that I'm real.

Everything, everything that my father has
ever told me about the unseen world—
      how Black people hold a magic
      so deep, so pure that he's spent

his entire life trying to understand it—
is right here in this house; right here in this kitchen.

And this magic is part of me.
Is this why my skin is my skin?

III

Lourdes leaves the kitchen, and
Kate and Dad are holding both of the twins,
who are quiet and wide-eyed.
The food is spread out to both ends
of the table and I'm not even hungry.
I don't even want to touch anything because
only the truth   can fill me up right now.

Elliott starts to cry in Dad's arms, as if
he can read my mind—
And Bethany starts crying, too, of course.

"I want you to enjoy your dinner, hon,"
Kate says. "Let Lourdes take care of them.
That's what she's here for."

Dad, while rocking Elliott in his arms,
takes a deep breath like he's inhaling
the whole house. "No. That's not what
she's here for, Kate," he says, seething.

And I sit up in my seat. This is it!
Dad is finally going to tell the truth!

"What do you mean this is not what she's here for?"
Kate says, glaring at my father while she nurses Bethany.
"I'm the one paying her salary . . ."

"I'm sorry, Kate," he says.
"But there's something I need to tell you . . . "

My ears perk up. Whatever happens,
I'll be taking Dad's side—
     And Lourdes's side.
     And my side.

But someone clears their throat, and we
all turn to see the girl standing in the
kitchen. "Excuse me. Do you need help
with the babies?" she asks.

Lourdes walks in behind her
as if they're tag-teaming on this.

Babies. My father's stories echo in
my mind: *The soucouyant or lougarou
shed their skin at night and fly around feeding
on the souls of babies,* he'd said.

I turn to Dad and look at baby Elliott
squirming in his arms. I remember what
happened that night. His tiny breath—
that feeling I had when I held him.

"We got it," I quickly say.
And I look at Lourdes—my mother.
    My mother?

But Kate says, "How about you both
join us? You've been such a wonderful
addition to our family these past couple
of weeks. I mean, Lourdes, I can't
thank you enough for all your help.
You and Marisol, please sit."

And then,   the girl—
I see her. I actually see her now
for who she might be—

Marisol.
She's Lourdes's daughter.
The eyes, the lips, the face, the skin—
It all comes down over me like a rainstorm.

So is she my   sister?   *My sister?*

My world explodes   and
I can't be here anymore.
I can't be here next to these people—
this mother   and daughter
whose flames   will burn me if
I don't leave   now.

Love

Never in this world
could I have ever imagined
that my family would
more than double—

Are we an actual family, though?
Especially if Kate doesn't know
what's going on. She believes
Dad's stories about shape-shifters,
werewolves, and vampires in the
Caribbean. But as an English professor,
they're just stories to her. Kate has said,
"Believing in stories doesn't make them
true, Daniel. Belief just gives people hope."

But hope is right here in this house.
For so long, I hoped for my mother.
For so long, I hoped to understand my skin.
Hope is magic made real—
Hope is the possibility of being something more
than human—

Still, my skin hurts to the touch.
Still, reality forces us to have to break bread

together and pretend to be only human.
Still, after all this time, I thought my mother was dead.
Still, as of two months ago, I thought the only
        siblings I had were Bethany and Elliott.
Still, I thought I was half mermaid made from silk.

Instead, I am half monster made from fire.
Instead, I have a sister who is
        a darker version of me.
Instead, my heart is expanding to a whole new reality,
        a whole new world is emerging,
        and one night, I will learn
        what kind of monster I really am—

But what do monsters do?
    What do lougarou and soucouyant—
    Caribbean shape-shifters and vampires do
    when the moon is new?

On the night of a new moon,
I've only watched the dancing elm on my ceiling.
And maybe I'll be the one dancing on
        my bedroom ceiling,
        a long-limbed and graceful
        chimera; a beautiful flaming monster
on the night of a new moon—

II

I couldn't eat. I couldn't just sit there
knowing that my father's secrets were
sitting around our kitchen table taking up
space like a looming dark cloud.
"I just *cannot* right now," is all I say
and push away from the table,
avoiding eye contact with everyone
and—

I pour myself into my homework
and block out the pain.
I pour myself into sending
stupid memes to Micah
and block out the pain.
I text Rena and Trish and
pretend everything is normal
and block out the pain.

But nighttime eases over my
world like an itchy, coarse blanket
and the pain becomes worse.

Hours after Dad's birthday dinner,
I'm supposed to be dead asleep.
But I know better than to try
to pretend that I can shut out
the world tonight; shut out the world

when everything,
including my body,   is on fire.

So I go up to my favorite place in this house,
where the sky will give me all the answers I need.

Dad sits on a lounge chair on the roof with
a glass of rum, his favorite. He's wrapped
in a chenille blanket Kate had gotten
him for Christmas and I wonder if he
really loves her after all—

Or is he still in love
with the other woman in this house?
The other woman in this house
who is helping take care of his babies.
The other woman in this house who,
just by looking at her, just by hearing
the sound of her voice, just by how
she can heal me with just one touch,
I know she is   my mother—

And there is no way I'll try
to explain all this to Micah.
He won't understand this hellfire
called my life—

So I ask my father to tell me his version

of my truth because
there are no storybooks for this—

III

"Hey, Gen," Dad says with his back to me
as he sits on one of the lounge chairs.

"Dad. You owe me a new story," I say,
not wanting to sit because everything
still hurts—
"You knew all this time what I am, what I'd become,
and let me believe that it was just a skin condition."

He'll tell me to put on a coat, but
my silk robe, Lourdes's coconut oil,
and being closer to the truth of who
and what I am are all healing balms
for my skin—

"Okay," he says, taking a sip from his glass.
"Gen. Hon. I wasn't sure what you'd become.
I mean, I am what I am. Human in mind, body,
and soul. It was supposed to happen at the onset
of puberty, but all you got when you were twelve
was bad acne. Nothing more than that. So maybe
you hadn't inherited any sort of   magic.

And I wasn't sure I believed any of it, until
your mother showed up—
Where do you want me to start this new story?"

I think of all the stories he's told me about
his trips to the Caribbean and why he got
into anthropology in the first place—

"Start from the beginning. What happened
when you went up to the mountains?" I ask,
because he's never really talked about it.
Only that he came down from the mountains
with a whole new understanding and passion for
                stories and the blurred lines
                between science and magic.

My father sets his glass of rum down
and I cautiously sit on a nearby chair
letting the cold winter air wrap its
soothing arms around me even though
it's nothing like Lourdes's embrace, and I stare
up at the waxing moon wondering how
many days it will be before it's new—

"We had paid a couple of the local guys
to drive us up the mountains to explore.
It was my twenty-fifth birthday. Me and

some of my college buddies at first—
good weed, good music, good vibes . . ."
My father starts his story—
"I met her on a beautiful new moon night.
Waves crashing on the shore below, steel pan
music, reggae, rum, a cool breeze from the ocean.
I remembered her from the resort—
She was the most beautiful thing
      I've ever laid my eyes on . . .
Later she would take my breath away. Literally.

"I asked her about this giant wooden
bowl she'd been carrying: a mortar without
a pestle. I asked about the carvings, and
she told me the stories of girls who shed their skin
to become meteors and comets and I believed
her.   I believed every single word.

And then she said . . ."

"Now that I told you, I will have to kill you,"
someone says from behind me.
I turn to see Lourdes without a coat, like me.
The night lights glow against her skin,
and she looks like a constellation—
"I knew you would not keep my secret.
I knew you would go and tell your buddies

about a shape-shifting girl you met
up in the mountains. . . ."

"But I never told them," Dad continues.
"I never said a word to them.
Not even when I got sick.
Fever, chills, night sweats, nightmares . . ."

"We do not kill," Lourdes says.
"We are not that kind."

"I knew what she did," my father says.
"The night hag. Old hag. Succubi.
The sleep paralysis demon.
The literal night mare.
But she came back. She came back to . . ."

"Heal him," Lourdes says.
"I needed his   help.
I wanted him to get me out of the Caribbean.
So we made a bargain,   but he wanted . . ."

"More. In exchange for papers, a visa, a passport,
I wanted her stories. I wanted to understand her.
But I fell   in love. I fell in love."

"He calls it love," Lourdes says, laughing a little.

"In order to understand me, he would have to
destroy me. In order to hear my stories,
I would have to destroy him—
And he called it love. Even while
proposing to his girlfriend, he called it love.
Even while marrying her at the resort where
I worked, he called it love. Even as I told him
I was with child, he called it love. And even
when he took my child from me and said he
could give her a better life, he called it love. . . ."

Lourdes steps closer to the edge of the roof
where a brick ledge separates us from our
brownstone and the night sky,   and
she doesn't face us as she speaks; she doesn't
look at me as she tells her version of my
                        origin story.

Dad gets up and walks to her, stands
beside her, and I'm here. I'm still here listening.
        "Dad," I say. "Is this true?"

The door leading to the roof from
downstairs slams shut behind me and,
the   girl   is   standing   there,   just   standing   there.

She doesn't have a coat on either.

                            "Mummy, is this true?"

she asks. And she walks up
to stand beside me as we both
wait   for answers from
my father and   her mother—

Our mother.

And tonight feels like a
     dead thing has been brought back to life,
     and its breath hangs low like the clouds,
     and with this new version of my
     origin story, maybe I will finally breathe too—

The girl,   Marisol,
     the nighttime version of me;
     the darker version of me,

takes my hand and holds it   like, she knew who I was
all along—

     a sister.

—MARISOL

Science

On the roof, I take Genevieve's hand
because I want her to know that she is not alone.
I have   a sister.   I have a sister!

And I am not alone.

I do not like her father, the collector.

He takes me and Mummy around
to see his collections and explains
to us our own story as if we don't
live it every day, every night,
and every new moon—

"Spontaneous human combustion has
been debunked by science," he says,
with his wire-framed glasses
slipping to the tip of his nose.
His hair hangs over his eyes,
and Mummy told me to be careful of
the scientists and scholars who will want
to destroy us in order to understand us.

I did not know,   I did not know
Mummy has been destroyed several times over,

so much so, that she gave this scientist

a daughter. His very own experiment.

II

I have a sister. I have a sister.

Mummy always knew I was never

Maria de la Soledad,

Our Lady of Solitude. She knew I was not

forever her only daughter;

forever a sole shooting star in the night sky.

And I am night and she is day.

Our faces are reflections of the same earth.

The sun rises on hers, the sun sets on mine—

But still we have only said

but a few words to each other.

One more week until the new moon—

So when Mummy and I are alone again,

and with my voice shaking and sadness

welling up in my eyes, I ask her,

"All this time, Mummy, you held an

empty space for this other daughter?

Is this why you brought us here?

To be the mother you never were to me?"

Mummy whispers, "I had to find her before
her very first shifting. I had to tell her the truth
of what she is. I have to guide her through it.
You know what will happen if she is alone."

I do. Without guidance, she will want
fresh souls. Babies. Her own siblings maybe.
But that is not my problem.
And I wonder who my mother will
want to enact revenge on now that she has
found the home she was searching for.

She is caring for babies—
We should never be so close to new life,
new breath on the night of the new moon—

GENEVIEVE—

Magic

On the night of the new moon,
something is supposed to happen
to me.   Something   big—

And Lourdes tells me she has to
make sure there's enough ice in
the house and I don't even know
what questions to ask other than

will it hurt—

And how do I build a bridge
between myself and this mother
who   gave me away to my father;
     gave me away to a country
     she didn't even know?
A mother
who   is teaching me how to become
     a nightmare—

I try to dream of the life I would've
lived had my mother kept me—

But the girl named Marisol is here
to remind me   that my mother

has another daughter   living the life
I could've lived—   She already knows
her power;   she already knows her magic.

"You can just quit," I tell Lourdes.
"You don't have to work here
anymore. Dad has money. He can
just give it to you."

Because I need her to make up for
        lost time.

"That is the same thing he offered me
before you were born," she says. "Money.
I gave him our stories. I gave him you."

My skin burns even more when she says this,
like, this is how my body is processing   truth.
And it's the first time I ever heard
those words to describe me; to describe my life—

Before I was born.

"My entire life   is   bargained   magic?"
 I ask. "I don't know who I hate more right now.
You or my father."

"Hey!" she hisses, and in the blink of an eye
she's right in front of me. Her breath is flames.
"You do not disrespect us like this. We gave
you life. Life!   You will never
understand all the bargains we make in order
to survive   where I come from. I gave you
more than life.   I gave you fulfilled dreams."

So I shrink down to an
obedient daughter, a version of me
I didn't even know existed.

What am I even supposed to do
with a monster for a mother?
Love her   or   fear her?

So when she puts the babies down
for the night, and Dad has started
drinking too much again, and Kate
is desperate to go back to work, and
the girl named Marisol hides in corners
thinking that I'm not watching her,
I ask, "Aren't you supposed to stay away
          from babies?"

I need her to tell me the   truth
because myth can also mean   lies—

"Everything on this planet feeds off
life force," she starts. "The trees from the air,
the flowers from the rain, the humans from the sun . . ."

"The monsters from the humans," I say.

"No. You've got it wrong," Lourdes says.
"The monsters from the monsters.
The humans from the humans.
The life force from the life force . . ."

"Babies, though?" I finally ask.

"Genevieve. It will take a lifetime
for you to understand."

"But I've already spent my whole life
not even knowing!" I say too loudly.
I don't care, because whatever
magic will happen on the new moon
will be an explosion of sound—
"And how are we supposed to keep
hiding this from Kate?"

"The same way we have been able to hide
this from the world." Lourdes says everything
with a smile, as if no question from me is too

stupid, as if she's thought of every possible
answer before I even ask. "Genevieve,
no matter how many books your father reads
or writes, no matter how many mortars he's
stolen from soucouyant, he will never be able
to understand or explain the
                                    incomprehensible.

"And you must soon learn how to shed this skin,
Genevieve. The skin that is given to you by them:
        mixed race, girl, middle-class, and American—
To wear the skin that is given to you by your foremothers:
powerful, cosmic, and   incomprehensible."

"Powerful, cosmic, and incomprehensible?"
I repeat. "When I feel so infuriatingly
        human?"
I can't wait for whatever will happen.
But at the same time, I need to be prepared
for what my mother monster says is
        the incomprehensible.

"Don't you worry your pretty head,
ma fille, my dear daughter—
Magic belongs to the soul
and not the mind."

Daughter. She called me daughter.
And now   I belong to something
other than nightmares and folktales—

II

And then she asks to do my hair—
I sit on the floor and rest my head
on her knee as she parts my thick,
curly strands and continues:

"When the tormentors reached
the shores of Africa and they
bargained with our chiefs
to steal our bodies,

  we were the first to burn—
Those of us who fought for our land,
  we were the first to burn—

Those of us who waged war
against the tormentors,
  we were the first to burn—

And our tormentors thought that
we would be withered to bone
and ash. But we rose out of the

flames, taking firelight with us
across the sky . . .

"And when we thought
our light would go out,
we returned to our tormentors,
one by one, and sipped from their
souls, taking back
        what is owed to us . . ."

Her voice is a sweet lullaby
even though her song is about war.

"My father never told me these stories,"
I say. "Men like him can be monsters too.
I've always known that I'm a descendant
of both slaves and tormentors."

She lets out a warm breath that
caresses the back of my neck, and
this makes my skin feel better.
"*Enslaved*," she says. "We were never slaves,
just like how we were never always monsters.
Monsters are born out of monstrosity.
Slavery was forced onto us.
So monstrosity was forced onto us."

My eyes are heavy, but it's not the
nightmares pulling back me into a dark place,
it's the memory   of all the monstrosities
that live in my DNA—

"How do monsters become   good?" I ask.

"There is only consequence, Genevieve.
And forgiveness. No good. No evil.
Just   consequences."

I could sleep while she braids
my hair and explains the incomprehensible,
but I don't—
And I've been awake since
the moment I learned the truth.
No nightmares, no dreams.
Only reality. But still,
everything hurts.
So I ask,   "Mama? Will I die?"

"Even vengeance must make way
for   forgiveness   and peace.
As long as there is war, as long
as there is cruelty, our flames will always
       burn bright," my mother says.

"You are still human, Genevieve.

Still made of skin. Except
instead of flesh and bone,
            we are fire and fury. . . ."

"And magic?" I ask.

"Story," she says. "Magic is story come to life."

Her healing fingers reach my scalp,
and even while my estranged mother's touch
is electric, I keep remembering Dad's words.
The soucouyant or the lougarou shed
their skin at night and fly around feeding
on the souls of babies—

If magic is a story come to life,
then will my father's stories come true?

The floor creaks outside my bedroom,
and Lourdes says, "Marisol? Is that you?"

At the same time, I hear Dad and Kate coming
in through the front door and the twins are crying.
And maybe I have to protect them from me;
I have to protect the twins from Lourdes;
I have to protect them from   my sister,
      Marisol,
on the night   of the new moon—

THREE

SISTER STARS

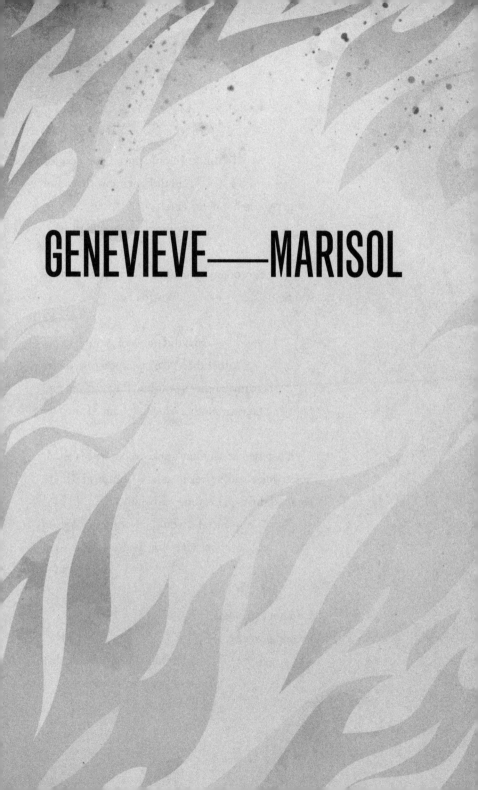

GENEVIEVE—MARISOL

Pretty

To think, I would have a princess for
a sister. And I did not know that a fire
could rage so hot in my core

without me even shifting—

Part of me—a small, growing part of me—
wants   to   destroy her.

She did not do anything to me
other than take my mother from me;
take my mother's braiding fingers from me;
take my mother's healing hands from me.

I listened as Mummy spoke to her with a much
softer voice, and I peeked at how Mummy lovingly
combed through her long curly hair,

and she would never do that for me
because mine is short and coarse
and—

I am not a princess.
I could never be.

Mummy never told me that
princesses can be monsters too—

We made fun of princesses at the resort.
They came with their sunscreen and tiny bikinis.
They asked us to take their photos by the pool
and on the beach and even after we returned
their phones and cameras, we never stopped
trying to capture their

                beauty in our memory—

       "Do you ever wish you could look
like them?" a sister soucouyant had asked
as we cleaned up after the princesses.
"Their long curly hair, their light bright skin,
their choice of any boy in the world . . ."

          "Every day," another one replied.
"Every   single   day."

       And when I first heard this, I wanted to cry.
There were soucouyant girls who use creams
to make their skin lighter. Burning a part of
themselves that already burns. They did not know
that it made the pain of shedding skin
and flying close to the rising sun

              that much more painful.

       And when one of the princesses fell ill,
we understood that vengeance

is a monster that can shape-shift too;
becoming   envy   and   greed
and all those emotions
that come with being   human.

So when Genevieve is downstairs,
I come upstairs. When she is upstairs,
I go downstairs. When she is in the front
of the house, I go to the back, avoiding
her and blending into the walls
like an old painting.
I wait until nightfall to eat
their leftovers; I tiptoe and whisper and
hide in the shadows of wooden sculptures
and masks that remind me of home.

But she is my mother's other daughter
and catches me when I'm not looking—

"We need to talk,"

Genevieve says.
She's at the top of the stairs
while I'm at the bottom.
She hovers, staring down
as if she already knows her power.

"So talk," I say.
She comes down,

I step back,
and we are face-to-face.

Her skin is almost
translucent
and the brown freckles
are like grains of sand
strewn across her
sunshine face.

"What's it like to be you?"

she asks.

Her warm breath stops mine
and it's odorless, as if it's my own.

"To have your mother with you?
To already know what you're made of?
To already know what you're capable of?"

"To be me? You want to know
my life?" I ask her.
"My life is like I am trapped
in a burning house and
my mother holds the torch.
Every new moon, she lets me out.
Every new moon, I'm summoned back."

Horror settles on Genevieve's
face, and she steps away.

"And you? What is it like
to be you?"
I don't really care to know,
but I am just making conversation.
I heard my mother
call this other girl
daughter—
I heard this other girl
call my mother
mama—

"To be me?"

she starts.

"You call it a house,
I call it my skin.
Except I didn't have a
mother to let me out
when it burns, until now—
I don't want it to be weird
between us. You probably didn't
have to share her with anybody."

"You can have her," I say.

"Why in the world would you say that
about your mother? At least you had one."

She walks past me
and leaves me standing there
sliced in half—

She takes the daughter part
of me to make herself
a whole child
with a mother and father
and a house made of magical stories—

A family.
A house.
A boyfriend.
A good school.

And this empty half of me
is still in this burning house
that is my life—

Three more nights
until the new moon—
But it can happen on any night
between now and then.

And we will both need
a tub or the mortar
　　　　to store our most valuable possession—
　　　　　　How will Mummy divide herself
between two daughters
　　　　　　　　as she keeps watch,
　　as she protects and guides
　　　　　　　　　our raging flames?

II

I don't know her like that. She doesn't
think I see her hiding, blending in with
all my father's art and trinkets. Her face is
like one of his many African masks
carved out of ebony—

But still, she's creepy.
And she's a　　　　　monster.
I don't know what a sister monster
　　will do to her own—

But Lourdes,　　　　my mother,
is boiling something smelly in the kitchen
while Dad and Kate are out showing off
the twins and Lourdes was asked to stay
here and cook and clean and I don't
have an opinion anymore about some

Black lady in our house because
    I want her here. I need her here.

She makes a warm compress—herbs
wrapped in white gauze—and places
it onto the red, burning parts
of my skin and it soothes the pain.
The swelling and rashes go down
and my face is clear, but I smell like
    ancient magic.

"Black castor oil and ancestor medicine," she says.
"I finally found the healing herbs that grow on the islands.
But this is only temporary—
The day before the new moon, you will have to let
    your skin do what it needs to do."

With every nice thing she does for me,
with every soft touch, with every gentle hug,
the different parts of me come together
at the seams, and I'm stitched
instead of patched; my wounds are healed
instead of suppressed—

"Mama," I say, just to hear the word
roll off my tongue so fluidly, like water;
    like ocean waves;   like a spell.

"Yes, my daughter," she whispers,
and looks into my eyes as if
    she's seeing me for the first time.

III

    I stand near the doorway leading
    into Genevieve's room and I watch
    as Mummy cares for her—
    I watch
    as Mummy makes the special compress
    for her—
    I watch
    as she births a whole other daughter
    two years older than me and I didn't
    know that I had taken space in a womb
that had already been   inhabited.

    Heat stirs in my belly, and Mummy
    always told me that human emotions
    will fuel my fire. But I held an empty
    space for Mummy to tell me what to
do with my rage;   her rage.

    "You are too young to have your
    own enemies, Mari," she'd said.
    "Whoever hurts you, hurts me.
    Whoever hurts me, hurts you."

And the walls to this house are
squeezing me in and
I   will   explode
before it is
time.

I can burn this whole place down
if I am not careful.

I want to say *Mama* too
so she can remember that
I   am   still here.

IV

I can't miss the dress rehearsal
for my upcoming performance—
Juilliard is on the line.
My future is on the line.
And I'm told nothing changes after
the night of the new moon.
Except   my power.

"I swear, there isn't a thing
Lourdes can't do!" Kate says
when I come down to the kitchen
before leaving for school.
"Your skin has cleared up again!

You are glowing this morning, Gen!"

I want to take her (rare) compliment
and throw it back in her face.
I wish I could tell her—
I wish I could just say that I'm a monster
and she better be careful what she says
to me or Dad from now on.

But Lourdes is here and I just tell Kate, "Thanks."

"We've got your performance on the calendar
for this weekend," Kate says. "But Lourdes asked for
some time off, so we'll be taking the twins to my sister's
in Manhattan. It was your father's idea to book a
hotel room nearby. Early Valentine's Day gift, I guess.
Our first date as parents!"

I glance at   my mother, Lourdes.
Dad   has already left for the day.
Dad   already knows what will happen.
Lourdes already planned how it will happen.
And   now I'm   split in two—

Girl   becoming.
Monster   becoming—

I want to tell the world
    what I am—
I want to show the world
    what I'll be able to do.

But I haven't even seen it for myself yet.

Marisol comes into the kitchen
and she's wearing the clothes I'd
put away into a donation bin
in the basement. Stupid middle school
outfits with too much lavender and pink.
She's wearing my past—
        and I don't want her to.

"Gen, Marisol will get to see you dance, right?"
Kate asks.
"Marisol, do you have a performing
arts talent? Maybe next year, you'll get into Gen's school."

V

        At the resorts, sometimes the nice tourists
           will slip a generous tip into our hand.
           I would split it with my soucouyant sisters
           and we would buy ourselves clothes in town.

Tight jeans, crop tops—any and everything
we see the princesses wearing.
Sometimes, the princesses would leave
behind their clothes and we take them—

So when Kate offered me
Genevieve's old clothes, I knew
I was also a   charity case.

"I don't know what you've already
learned at your old school on the islands. Maybe
they should've held you back a grade or two,"
Kate had said. "Let's see. What's the last
novel you've read, Marisol?"

I don't know what Mummy has told her
about my education, but I am not stupid.
I showed her the tattered pages of the
book I've been reading since
we arrived in New York.
"Four times in one month," I said.

She gasped and took the book from me
as if it is a precious thing.
"Morrison's *The Bluest Eye*. Of course
you would love that book!
I can't get Genevieve to read anything
other than horror and fantasy."

"I like   reality," I said.

"Well, reality can be so sad sometimes."

Kate smiles at me as if I am her student,
but there is nothing she can teach me.

And Mummy is proud when she sees me
wearing a new-to-me outfit, decent clothes,
          and not the nightclub clothes
          she made me leave behind.

But I only chose a pair of sweatpants and
          a purple-and-pink sweater
because those were the only clothes that fit;
          and the colors remind
          me of home—the bright bungalows,
the turquoise ocean, the hibiscus bushes,
          the yellow sunshine
          Genevieve's old clothes—
And now she only wears black.

          I finally own a coat.
          Genevieve's old coat.

"Yes, I have many performing talents,"
I say with an attitude, and I am sure
          that Genevieve wants to tell

Kate about herself too.

"Do you like your   mother?"
I ask Genevieve when we're both
out of the house and she's
pacing quickly in front of me.
The words had already spilled
out of my mouth by the time
I realized what I had just asked her.

VI

What am I, her babysitter?

Kate is in on this. She has to know
what's going on; she has to know
who Lourdes and Marisol really are
or else why would she have me out
here babysitting this girl?

Who would've ever thought a year
ago that I'd be a big sister, not to
just twin babies, but to a whole other
girl—this nighttime version of me.

My world is falling apart and coming
together all at the same time, and I'm

right in the middle, doing shit like
walking a new little sister to school.

My old clothes are tight on her.
That coat is out of style.
Her hair is like a boy's. She needs
some braids, a wig, a weave—
something. And some lip gloss too.
Mascara, liner—a whole makeover.
I know what girls who look like her
have to do to look   decent.

But I just say, "My mother? I don't
know if it's true. I need a DNA test."

She walks a little bit behind me and
I move fast, not wanting to be late
or   not wanting to be seen with her.

And she says,

       "I meant Kate. But okay. You are talking about
          Lourdes, *my* mother. And a test for what?
            Didn't Mummy tell you that science
              can't prove what we are?"

"I still need proof," I say, and it's a lie.
I'm not ready to have this conversation

with her. I'm not ready to let her think
that I'm so gullible to believe that a
woman can just walk into my life and claim
to be my mother, and that my skin is this bad
because I'll be shifting out of it in a few nights
to become a flying fireball witch—
I pretend to be unbothered—a mask and a shield.

I thought we would have to ease
into this discussion of being sisters
and all, but it is clear she still has doubts.
"Well, you will find out soon enough.
I hope it will be all the proof in the world,"
I say, and it is not my job to
convince her of anything—

I try not to stare at my sister for too long.
She wears shiny lip gloss. Her big, curly hair frames
her face like a portrait. Her lashes almost touch her
eyebrows and her cheekbones are high like

mine and Mummy's. Kate is right. She is glowing.
She will glow even more after her first shedding.
But not in the way that she thinks;
not in the way that she will want, maybe.

She has her mother's singsong lilt.
And I can't deny it. She *is* my sister.

I don't need a test, but still—
I need to hold on to some version of
reality where this sort of thing is wild.
And Micah is the only person
who will make me feel like
my feet are still grounded here in
Brooklyn, in New York, in this country,
on this planet. So I tell Marisol,

"I don't know if I believe that magic
is always beneath the surface of
everything.   *Everything.*"

She shoots me a sneaky grin
and it's like I'm seeing my own face
reflected back to me—except darker.

                    I don't want to talk about magic
                            because going to school
                    is a reality I want to live in, so I ask,
                        "Do you like your   school?"

"I love my school," I say, and   maybe
we can at least be   friends.
"But my dad hates it. If you ask me, I think
it's because there's too many Black kids.
He thinks it's *subpar*. But the other schools in
the building are worse. That's where you're going.

Micah's school. I'll tell him to look out for you."

And there he is, waiting for me at the corner
wearing that big, bright smile. His dark,
chiseled face is like my father's
African masks too, and I managed to
get the best-looking basketball player
in all of Flatbush—
Today, I won't hide from him.
My skin is fine, for now.
My makeup is perfect, for now.
I feel   normal, for now.
So when I reach Micah, he opens
his arms wide and hugs me tight
and kisses my forehead so gently.
Nothing hurts,   for now.

"I missed you," he whispers
into my ear. And he takes my hand
as we walk to school like we always do;
like this is the reality I've always
known, and I forget for a moment that
it's two more nights until—

Ugly

The night of the new moon, I will
have to find my own sustenance;
find my own vengeance. And seeing
his face, remembering his voice
calling me ugly reminds me of
what I have to do—

How could they not remember me?
How could they not have seen me?
A few weeks ago, I was just a nameless
ugly face; a body to push to the ground
and discard like the garbage on the street.

I am both invisible and too visible;
transparent and opaque at the same time.

So I walk behind Genevieve
and her boyfriend and she doesn't know—

She doesn't know that she will have to make
enemies; she will have to find vengeance too.

She thinks   this is love—

I slow my pace when we get close

to the bakery. Genevieve looks back
at me and motions towards the door.
And there it is—

A photo of Mummy is taped to the glass
with the word *LOUGAROU* in big red letters.

My fireblood boils. How dare she?
How dare Jean-Pierre's wife make such
a public accusation? I hope the customers
don't believe her. I hope they've really forgotten
their island superstitions to even think that
this   is   true—

Then Micah takes Genevieve's hand
and pulls her into the bakery. She looks
back at me with worried eyes.
What does she want me to do?

"Let me get you something to eat before
your dress rehearsal," I hear Micah say.

And he must've seen that photo.
He must've seen my mother
at Genevieve's house.
But he walks right into
the bakery with Genevieve
on his arm and I stay outside

because because
that place   is a graveyard
holding dead memories
                of a time me and Mummy had to
survive—

              So I hide my face as I pass the bakery
                        to get to the school—
              Customers are coming in and out.
              The workers are back, which means

                    Jean-Pierre is feeling better,
                    and I hope he learned his lesson.
                    Jaden is behind the register and

        Madame Jean-Pierre is nowhere in sight.
              Then I realize I have an abundance
              of options—a menu to choose from

                    for the night of the new moon.

                    Micah for calling me ugly—

              Madame Jean-Pierre for putting up
                    that photo of my mother and
                        forcing us to leave—

                    Kate?   Daniel?

And—
I've tried to do it before,
lock my mother out.
What would life be like
without her? If I don't let her
return to her skin, I can just start my
own life, live my own dreams,
chart my own path in the night sky,
and become my own constellation
on the night of the new moon—

II

That picture of Lourdes is still there
and it's been weeks. Micah has seen it.
And he's seen Lourdes at my house—
but according to him, he doesn't
believe in those things. But still
I pull the photo off the door on my
way in, and Micah is distracted
by the array of fresh bread and pastries
on display behind the counters.

The place is buzzing with customers,
including some kids from our school.
A couple of girls are in line and Micah
pulls away from me to check out the
drinks in the fridge and the same boy

who was here last time steps
out from behind the counter,
brushes past me, and whispers,
"I've seen him come in with one
of those girls. You deserve better."

His warm breath, his words like soft cotton
against my cheek makes my skin feel like it's
lighting up with tiny, shimmering lights.
For a second,   nothing hurts.

Not even Micah. Not even Micah
does   this   to me—

I glance over at Micah, who is chatting
with the girls now, and my insides heat up,
simmer, come to a boil and this feels
worse than what happens to my   skin.
I clench my fist and ball up the photo,
and pretend I'm holding Micah's
entire soul in my hand—

Rena told me.   Trish warned me.
Micah   is a cheater
and I didn't think;   I didn't think
he would ever cheat on me—
Why would he?

So when he comes back to
the counter, I whisper, "You know them?"

"Yeah," he says, looking at me sideways
like I'm supposed to be minding my business.

"Are you checking out those girls?"
I ask him straight up, just as the boy
from behind the counter walks out
of the bakery, like he knows he instigated
this shit—

                    "Marisol!" someone calls out from behind
                    me, and I freeze. Jaden. He saw me.
                    I could just keep walking, but
                    his voice is a magnet pulling
                    me back to some feeling
                    I cannot name.
                    He is still forbidden—

                    But I turn around and smile.
                    He waves me over. I shake my head.

                    "She's upstairs," he mouths, pointing up.
                    He's talking about Madame Jean-Pierre,
                    but I can't risk her seeing me in the bakery.
                    He calls me over again.

And Genevieve and Micah are still
in there. And maybe he has news
about Jean-Pierre's condition,
or he has something to tell me
about what people are saying
about my mother—

So I rush to Jaden only for him to say,
"You gonna walk past and not say hi?"

"Jaden, please. You have my mother's
picture on the door, and she had nothing
to do with Jean-Pierre being sick."

And Jaden says, "I always knew it was you."

My stomach twists.
And magic folk can always sniff
how the air bends around us just so—

He pulls me into the bakery,
where Genevieve and Micah
are at the counter waiting to order
and the picture of my mother is gone.
I glance down to see Genevieve
balling up a paper in her hand—
Good. She is protecting our mother.

Even so, I can't be seen here.
My heart races because
any one of the customers
can point a finger accusing me
of what I did to Jean-Pierre.
And this time, it will be true.
I can't have Madame Jean-Pierre
making a scene in front of Genevieve
and her boyfriend—

To be called what we really are
is a cross we bear, is a skin we wear—

And now, in this moment,
I don't want to be incomprehensible.
Would it be so bad to just be
Black, girl, immigrant?

But not ugly. Never ugly.

Micah turns and looks
straight into my eyes and asks,
"You want something, Marisol?
I know you're from the islands too.
What's your favorite?"

"Um," I stutter   because   because
he doesn't know

that I was the girl he called ugly—
"Coconut bake," and my words
fall out like crushed ice.

I drop my head and want to
hide again.

The boy behind the counter
slipped a little something extra
into my white paper bag. I don't know
if I should be having gluten or anything
sweet before my dress rehearsal,
but I could eat this entire bakery.
This hunger feels brand-new
and it's like a hole is widening inside of me
and it wants   the world—

"Sweets for the sweet," the boy whispers,
just as Micah is saying something to Marisol.

Micah is being fake right now just 'cause I asked
him a simple question. *Were you checking out*
that girl?

"What's your name?" I ask the boy as he
puts coconut bake in the bag.

"Jaden," he says, smiling, as that black cat

leaps onto the counter, introducing itself too.
Jaden is not nearly as cute as Micah, but
I bet he would treat me better.
I bet he would treat other people better.

The two girls who are flirting with Micah
are from his school and I can't believe
he's actually flirting back, and they don't
care that I'm standing right here.
I'm standing right here!

They brush past me and lock eyes with Micah
and I stare them down wishing that I could
say something; do something   because
I didn't think that   I didn't think that
jealousy could be a rage   so hot;
hotter than how my skin gets on
some nights and I know for sure,   I know in
my core   that anger is a very
dangerous thing   for monsters like me.

But is this the right anger, though?
I'm mad 'cause Micah is talking to some pretty girls?
Still, I can't   suppress this   fire—

                              Two girls walk out of the bakery
                              while giggling and saying bye to

Micah as if they are sharing
a secret joke. Genevieve glares at
them and it is clear that she
already has enemies.   Good.

I already feel sorry for those girls.

III

We are steps from the school
where Micah had tripped me and he
wraps his arm around my sister's neck
like she is his property.

I know this song. I know this rhythm—
The men who come to the resorts slip
a few American dollars into our hand
and think they   own us.
I wonder how much Daniel had slipped
into Mummy's hand. It does not matter,
because she gave him something priceless—
a magical daughter.

And everyone gathers around Genevieve
like moths to a flame—
I know this song. I know this rhythm.
We have names for girls

like her on the islands.
Princess. Supermodel.
Red gyal. Browning. Grimelle. Mulatresse.

And when they call us
blackie
it's worse than being called a monster.

And the new-fallen snow is white
against the gray concrete—
And the muted sun is yellow
against the powder-blue sky—
And I am dark brown against
everything that glitters—

including my new sister.

Micah looks back at me
and furrows his brow. I am devouring
the coconut bake Jaden had given me
because before the new moon,
hunger is a bottomless pit I can
never fill up with bread—
Soon, I will need to sip from
a soul—
I make myself into a shadow and

Micah says something to Genevieve and
she   laughs and   laughs and—

The sound echoes all around like a nightmare.

Ugly   ugly   ugly   ugly   ugly   ugly

is a word I have heard all my life;
is how I feel when the world holds up
its princesses as if they are the stars
that make up constellations;
is what I become
on the night of the new moon;
is what Genevieve will be too
on the night of the new moon—

Micah is nice   until he is not.
He is like the boys who lure us with sweets
only to laugh when we come back for more.
I should not have been so surprised
by his small gesture—

"Oh, that's my cousin!"

Genevieve says
loud enough for me to hear,
just as two girls are approaching.
They are both a dark and light princess

with their long hair and made-up faces
and disapproving eyes—

Did she just call me her cousin?

Micah's jokes are never funny,
especially not when he's making
fun of my sister like that—
I don't tell him that's who she is, of course,
but I don't ignore Marisol, neither.

So when Trish and Rena start walking
towards us, I start to laugh like I always do.
Them seeing me happy is the sweetest revenge
for all the hate they've been throwing my way—

And everything I do around them is to never
let them know that I am always, always in pain.
Mind, body, and soul—
Except for this morning.
So I laugh extra hard and pull Marisol into
my life like she's always been there—

"Yeah, my cousin," I say, when Trish
asks again, like she can't believe I have
a Black cousin. "Y'all know my mother's Black,
right? She's from her side of the family and she's

staying with us for a while. She'll be going to
   Micah's school."

I shoot Marisol a look, and even though we're
still getting to know each other, I hope she
can understand sister code. Like, just go along
with it until I can explain—

"Cool," is all Rena and Trish say, and I bet they
believe me now. And I keep Marisol close
because she is helping me prove that I am
what I am.   Here, she'll be my cousin.
Distant but still close. Blood, but only half.
Nothing more. Nothing less—

         And I keep Genevieve's secret for her.
           If she wants me to be her cousin,
        then it's better than explaining to her
        friends that her mother has seemingly
        come back from the dead and brought
           another daughter with her—

          I get it. Sometimes the myth
            is better than reality.

IV

The Black girls in my dance class
are putting on a Black History Month
performance and Rena and Trish
were trying to keep me out—

The Black girls in my dance class
wanted each of us to choreograph an
homage to Black women pioneers
and they have left me out—

So I begged the teacher for a solo and
Kate sent an email and Dad spoke to the
head of the dance department and
    now I have my solo
for the Black History Month performance.

I've been working on it for months—
A contemporary piece to
Beyoncé's "Pretty Hurts,"
and maybe this was when
things started getting weird with
Rena and Trish—

Our dress rehearsal will be during
second period and we're performing
for the whole school before tomorrow's opening night,
and I need everything to be   perfect.

I need my skin calm, my fires put out, my rage cooled,
my life normal   just until I get through
my performances. And Lourdes never explained to me
what will really happen before and after the
night   of the   new moon—

V

Not even carnival season on the islands
is this chaotic. With so many people
smashed up against each other as they
march and dance on the road, we should
be afraid of guns and knives and fights.
No—
Even our own governments trust us to be
civilized during the most hectic time of the year.

Here, they do not even trust their students—
They seem to think that kids my age are a
threat to humanity itself. It is as if I am going
through airport security with the metal detectors
and ID checks and suspicion and scrutiny.

Genevieve and I had to walk in through
different doors of the same building.
I can tell by the color
of some of the students' skins
which school they are attending.

Genevieve takes an elevator
to the top floor—

My first class is English
and I hold my head down
as I walk to the back
of the classroom
as quiet as smoke—

Here, the colors are like dusk,
even though it's morning
the sun has already set on
the kids who look like me—
Our brown skins blend into the grays,
blend into the blacks,
blend into the background
like long-cast shadows—

But still,
it's hard not to notice the sun
when it sets.

And we make music with our entire souls.
"Why do you think Hurston used dialect
in her novel?" the teacher asks
about the book we're reading,

Their Eyes Were Watching God,
and her undulating words let me know
that she's from the islands too.

She is a mirror for us—
So I round out the corners of my sentences
and this classroom feels like home.
"Because dialect is like a second skin
and it's the magic we wield in our words,"
I say without raising my hand.

And when the teacher smiles,
the sun finally rises in this classroom.
"That's so beautifully said, Marisol."

And I smile back to greet the sun.

And, maybe, my American dream
is to peel away the layers of our magic
one beautiful metaphor at a time—

VI

Lines of kids
pack into the hallway and I'm told there
is a special Black History Month assembly.

Micah passes me in the hall.
He walks as if he owns every corner
of this building. Even the teachers and
security guards yield to his presence.
"Hey, cuz!" he says with a bright smile
and he is not the sun—
"Gen's performing. You coming?"

And soon I am pulled into a group
of boys who are as tall as mapou trees.
They laugh and joke and I wonder
when they will turn their attention to me.

Micah makes me sit next to him and
maybe I am just a mascot for now—

"You sure she's Gen's cousin?" a boy
asks, and I do not even look his way
to see what kind of face he is making.

Micah laughs, and I soon realize
that I am an inside joke.
"Yeah!" he says. "Isn't that wild?"

I laugh too because I can't hold the truth
any longer. "What is even wilder
is that I am actually—"

"May I have your attention please!" a teacher
shouts from the front of the auditorium,
and she cuts me off—

Everyone fidgets in their seats and the
place is electric with excitement.

"My baby's gonna kill it!" Micah says.

After two teachers and the principal
shout into a microphone for everyone to
settle down; after a girl walks
onto the stage to announce the
theme of the performance
(badass Black women in history)
and everyone cheers;
after Genevieve's friends and
two other girls dance to a sorrowful
song about racism and freedom
while wearing flowing white dresses—

And my heart almost leaps out of my
chest because their dance is so beautiful,
it conjures spirits and memory—
And those girls don't know,
they don't know that dancing for the
ancestors is where magic is born—
Even humans can harness their

invisible magic with just their bodies;
with just their voices.

I remember the names of the women they
dance for: Harriet Tubman, Ida B. Wells,
Queen Nanny of the Maroons,
and Queen Anacaona of Hispaniola.

They tell the stories of these women with
their entire bodies, their entire souls, and I wish
so badly that I could do the same for all the
soucouyant and lougarou women who
were born out of war;
out of pain;

out of slavery.

It feels like I am the only one who
wants to stand and applaud
because the entire auditorium
is quiet as if they have just listened to
a boring speech—

It is Genevieve's turn to dance.
When she walks onto the stage
everyone cheers as if she is
a superstar; as if she is the one
they have been waiting for—
She is barely dressed

in shorts and a bra that look
like underwear.
Her body is sculpted—
Her slight curves and sharp angles
are made for moving like the wind;
are made for flying—

I can't see how something so beautiful
will have to shift into something so gruesome
and I know   I know that this is
what makes us   incomprehensible.

And I did not know   I did not know
that my sister is a
superstar—

VII

Micah's school is the first to come
into the auditorium, and there's enough
space to seat the whole neighborhood.

Since we're the only performing arts
school in the building, we're supposed
to put on a show for all the students
before performing for family and friends.
This is what I love about being here.
I'm not dancing for a bunch of stuffy

white people who clap like robots
and who'll get offended if I twerk—

Too bad I didn't inherit Lourdes's and Marisol's
curves, but still I work with what I got.
Micah is always my biggest fan—
and he's front and center with his
boys, his teammates,   and

Marisol is sitting right next to him—
My belly is in knots.

Lourdes never told me that
human emotions can still take up space
in my soul.   How do monsters
conquer fear?   How do monsters
conquer insecurity?   How do monsters
dance like the world is on fire and all they
want to do is   kiss the sun?

                    When the light shines on Genevieve
            she looks like
            the moon
            and sun
            and stars

                                    colliding—

Every part of my body has to interpret
every word to the song—
Pretty   hurts.
I had to fight for my right to be on this stage—
I know for sure that I have a history too—
And I can be the hero in my own story
because through all the pain,
          through all the uncertainty,
          through discovering what I am,

I   can still dance like my life
depends on it.   It does. It really does.
Sweat starts to form on my skin and slowly,
slowly everything begins to   burn again.
The heat surfaces and maybe I become smoke.
And my heart   my heart feels like it's igniting
everything.   And I'm hot, hot, hot.
The light is shining on my skin
     and maybe everyone can
     see the little fires on my body—
But still, I don't stop. I don't let myself cool down.
Every move is my shout into the wind.
Every kick, every extension, every spin
is my soul   yelling to the sky.
Pretty   hurts.
Pretty   hurts.
Pretty   hurts—

Micah and the boys   Micah and the boys
gawk at Genevieve as if she is a
rocket ship launching into space—

And her performance is not a sports game.
But they whoop and cheer
with every move Genevieve makes.

And she is the rotating universe—

That is what I feel in my belly.
Rage   stirs and stirs
and I am   hot   hot   hot—

Mummy has taught me to name what I feel.
Mummy has taught me to let my fire burn
so it can launch me across the sky.

And I shrink in my seat because   because
I want this   I want this
for myself—

To be able to dance like that.
To be able to look like that.
To be able to have an audience full of people
cheer and applaud me as if I am creating

the universe over and over again
with just my soul; with just my skin—

In this moment, I don't care about shape-shifting.
I don't care about being able to inhale souls.
I don't care to be a comet or a meteor in the night sky.

I want to be comprehended. I need to be understood.
I   want   to be   celebrated—

Human.   Girl.   Pretty.
                                                  Pretty.
                                                  Pretty.

Genevieve   has that power.

And I am the only one left sitting
            after   my sister
gets a   standing ovation—

Pretty hurts?
How is pretty a painful thing?

GENEVIEVEMARISOL

Smoke

The school nurse came backstage
because after my performance,
my skin flared up so bad, they
thought I was having an allergic
reaction.   Everyone must've
noticed, but still they applauded;
but still they stood up for me and
made me feel   like   the sun—

Micah was the only one who came
rushing to me—
I turned him away. I don't want him to see me like this.

So I asked for Marisol;   I begged for her to
come backstage   even though she was
supposed to go to her next class;
                        even though no one
     believed that we are related.

I needed her—I needed her by my side.
So I said, "She's my sister; my half sister."
And they still didn't believe me—

But she came on her own.
She came to   rescue me—

I'm hiding in the dressing room.
Marisol helps me with my clothes,
carefully avoiding the sore and red spots.

"Do that thing your mother does," I whisper.

                              "I came to see if you are okay,
                                        but have to be in class,"
Marisol says, and I can't believe she's not
going to   help me—

                    "I have to go to biology and math, and . . .
                        I have to be in school, Genevieve."

"School isn't going anywhere,
but it feels like I'm dying over here and
you're not going to help me?
        When will this   stop?"

                    "Soon. It will all be better soon. But I need to go
                to school.   My mother can help you, not me."

"Don't let me go through this alone, Marisol."
I grab her hand and when I touch her, it doesn't
hurt. Her skin is cool against mine, and something
electric is exchanged between us. She tries to pull
away but I hold tight and don't let go—
"Come back home with me. I can't be here.

I have to be better for tonight's performance.
My skin has to clear up again. Help me."

                I feel the energy draining from me.
    as if she is   taking small sips
                    from my life—
      There's nothing I have that she would want,
    except   our mother.

                  She finally lets me go.
    But not really—
       I am bound to her; tethered at the soul.

                  I want to stay in school.
        I have not even taken my first exam
              to prove my intelligence;
    to prove that I am
                comprehensible—

                  And now, I am once
        again in service to a princess.

II

She comes home with me.
Maybe it was because of the way I cried.
Maybe it was because of the way I held

her hand so tight, our souls must've melded.
No one is home and I call my dad, but
he doesn't pick up.
I call Kate, but she doesn't pick up.
They've already left to go to Kate's
sister's apartment with the twins.
This all must've been Lourdes's idea.

"Where's your mother?
What is she planning to do to the twins?"
are the first questions I ask—

                              "What are you accusing my mother of?"
Marisol says, and I've pissed her off.
She knows why. She knows the stories.
She knows the truth—
"I have to protect my brother and sister from . . ."

                              "From what? From who?"

"Why did your mother have to take the
weekend off? She must've wanted them
out of the house for a reason. Are the babies
easier to get to in someone else's apartment?
Tell me the truth, Marisol!"

                    I knew it. I knew it was only a matter of time.

I left school and came back home with her.

I surrendered to her tears.

I surrendered to her tight grip on my hand

because I am all she has right now.

I am loyal to my fellow soucouyant,

sisters by flame—

And I want to feel sorry for her. I want to feel

something other than   envy.

"We   are   not   that kind!"

I say through clenched teeth.

I have startled her.

She tenses up and steps back.

"I hate when people

accuse us of that. Not everything

in our stories is true."

"Am I   that kind?"

she asks.

I don't respond because it's a

question only she can answer.

She will know soon enough

what kind of monster she really is—

"The cool air will help," I tell her.
"I can't do what my mother can do.
That takes years of shifting and flying
to be able to harness the healing
powers of the sun. My hands
are just my hands."

"But I felt something—
like a shot of electricity,"

she says,
and tries to take my hand again.
I don't let her.

She is trembling. She is holding her arms
away from her torso as if her own body is
turning against her—
That is what happens to us when we shift.
Our skins become our enemy, and she will
have to learn this on her own.

"Genevieve, the only way to understand
what is happening to you is to surrender,"
I say. "Didn't Mummy tell you that the self
that is inside is not the self that is outside?
Your firesoul has a mind of its own. And it
wants to get out. It is hungry and it will
have to feed itself."

I want to tell her that I'm scared.
I want to tell her that I don't trust
the one person who can really help me right now.
I want to keep telling her that this hurts
like hell. But she already knows—
She knows what this feels like and she's not
helping me.   It's almost as if she wants
to see me suffer through this—

It's still the middle of the day and this is the
worst I've ever felt. The only place in this
house that brings me some relief is the roof.
"Did it hurt this bad for you?" I ask Marisol
because she is so close, hovering, and
I wonder if she's laughing at my pain.

                    Genevieve's skin is an erupting volcano—
              I have been through this.

                          I have seen girls go through this.
                          But they have never been so light;
                                    never half white.

                                    So I say,
              "Our dark skin is both a shield
              and a source of power—

                          Our dark skin is what fuels
              our flames.

Our dark skin is
magic inherited

and magic wielded."

"Dark skin?" I turn to look her in the face.
"My skin is   not like yours, Marisol."

"Then maybe you're not really one of us,"
I say, and it's a lie I want to believe.

How could she be?
How could she be like us
when she was raised so far
away from our sun;
so far away from the
stories that rule our

magic, our power?
How could she be when she is
half tormentor and half tormented?

I get a glass of ice from the kitchen,
a small towel dampened with cold water,
and Mummy's Bible from our bedroom.
Nothing more. Nothing less.

It is still daytime and it's as if
she is in labor and is about to

give birth to her monster self—

III

I want to strip naked, but she's still here.
I keep my clothes on even though the
fabric feels like tiny needles poking my skin.
I clench my fists and clench my jaw and bear it.

                              "You have to breathe through it,"
Marisol says.

                    "Do not tighten your body or it will feel worse.
                              Make your skin like air, like water."

"How do you know?
How do you know what I'm supposed to do
when I'm not your kind. Huh, Marisol?"

                                        "I'm trying to help, Genevieve.
                              You want to live through this, don't you?"

"Live through this?
When it feels like I'm dying?"

                                        "Yes. A part of you is dying so a
                              new part of you can live. Every new moon,
                                        you will have to rebirth yourself,

and someone will have to pay the price
for your soucouyant life,"
I tell her. Then, after she doubles over
taking short, quick firebreaths, I say,
"Micah hasn't been kind to you."

I hope my words will guide her firesoul,
like Mummy's words guide mine.
"Micah hasn't been kind to you," I repeat.

My security blanket has always been the
night sky, but it's still the middle of the day
and Marisol is up on this roof with me
with a glass of ice, a towel, and a Bible,
and she says that Micah hasn't been kind to me,
but   what does she know about me and Micah?
"What's that supposed to do?" I ask, pointing to
        the Bible.

                              "Mummy prays through it."

"Like, to God?"

                              "Yes, who else do you think?
                              She is not going to pray to the devil."

"I mean, we *are* monsters, right?"

I hiss, because even my words,
even my thoughts seem to ignite the burning.

> "No. We are not the kind of monsters
> that destroy the world. We are not the
> kind of monsters that seek power
> for power's sake—"

Marisol says this as if I've offended her,
offended us. So I ask, "What kind then?"

> "The kind of monsters that are made,
> not born,"

she says, almost whispering.

> "I think we will spend our whole lives
> trying to figure out if we are good
> or if we are bad—

They call us   monsters,
but   we are necessary.
They call us   evil,
but   we are misunderstood.
> The only thing that is true
is that we are   here.
We are ugly   but we are here—

> Fire destroys and fire nourishes.

We are human too, Genevieve.

Do not ever forget that."

"What will happen to the person
I go after?"

"Your soucouyant self will know what to do,
like how babies know how to   survive."

"Will my skin get better?"

She looks me up and down
and I don't hide myself from her
the same way I've been hiding from everyone else.
And maybe, she's the only person in the world
who'll get me   if I'm honest with her;
if she's honest   with me—

IV

"It depends on what you mean by better,"

I tell her, because soucouyant

are daughters of the night,

kissed by the sun.

"Clear and smooth and   pain free,
like yours,"

she says, inching closer to me now, as if
she wants to touch my face.

I dare her.
"You do not know what happens when things
burn?" I ask. "How fire scorches everything
that it touches? How the flames lick your skin
and you become darker than the night?"

"Darker than the night?"

she asks, wrinkling her forehead
because she will never understand
these truths until she experiences it
for herself; until she goes through
the fire herself.

Soon now. Soon—

"I was twelve when I first shifted,"
I tell her, as we both stand on the roof
looking out over the streets,
and it is covered in a blanket of snow.
I am not impressed with this view.

I'm convinced   that white
is the color of death.
It envelops everything in this

city as if the entire place
is mourning—

"What did it feel like?"

she asks.
"Like I was dying. Like I could eat
the world. Pain and hunger and rage
all at the same time," I say, remembering
the worst night of my life.

It was also the best night of my life.
I don't tell her that after the first
shifting, she will return to her skin
feeling like she can inhale the universe
and that sort of power, that sort of freedom
is inexplicable—

V

"Dad, where are you?"
I shout into the phone. "It's happening!"

I'm on the roof—
I'm on the roof stripped down to my
rawest self.   It's nighttime now, and I was
supposed to have stayed at school

to rehearse for tonight's performance
but   I'm on the roof—
I'm on the roof stripped down to my
rawest self.   And Marisol is pacing,
still holding that glass of ice,
still holding that Bible,
still not doing anything to
                               help me!

I'm on the roof   I'm on the roof
stripped down to my rawest self—

"Gen, we took the twins to
Kate's sister's apartment. Kate and I
will be at a hotel. Lourdes . . . she told me
to stay away. She threatened me. . . . I can't be there
with you, hon.   But you're safe.
She is the only one in the world who
can help you. I'm sorry, hon,"
my father says, and his voice is distant,
like he left me out here. He knew this was going
to happen and he left me out here   alone.

"Then where is she? She's not here!"
I shout into the phone.

"Is Marisol with you?" he asks.

I don't answer him and hang up.
I want   the woman who made me
like this. I want the father who knew
I was like this—

VI

The moon, like everything else
in this universe, is predictable.
Its phases affect the tides and our cycles
and can drown us in our own tears
if we are not careful—

The sun, like everything else
in this universe, is predictable.
It gives us life and can start
heat waves and scorch the earth
if we are not careful—

The stars, like everything else
in this universe, are predictable.
They can implode and become a
supernova consuming everything
in their path, including us
if we are not careful—

So with Genevieve, I am careful.

It's not supposed to be time yet,
but I can tell by the way her skin
is erupting that her infant
soucouyant self is ready to
break   out.
The new moon calls us on any one of the
three nights between its waning and waxing—

And Genevieve does not know,
she does not know that her time has come—

Where is Mummy?
Where is she to guide this daughter
of hers? Where is she to pray
and conjure the monster out of her;
to talk   the fire   out?

And as I watch Genevieve writhe her body
in pain, I start to feel the tingling
beneath my own skin   too—

GENEVMIEAVREISOL

Mirror

The cold isn't enough.
The roof isn't enough.
Marisol's vague answers aren't enough.

"I need the mortar," I tell her.

        "No! That mortar belongs to my mother,"
she says with wide eyes,
like I just asked for the most
forbidden thing—

"I can use one of Dad's.
The stories say I need a mortar.
Where's my mortar?"

        "No, no, no, no, Genevieve! There are rules.
        There is protocol. There is respect.
        The tub will do. That is what I use."

        She is being a princess right now and
        she doesn't know how to make do
        with what we have. Yes, we are magical,
but this is not a storybook.
        This is real, and she will soon learn

that there can be scarcity in magic;
there can be poverty in power.

Still, her bathroom is beautiful
and she does not have to shift in a
stained tub, in a decrepit apartment, like I did.

This isn't what I thought my first shifting
would be—alone with my half sister.
No community of girls and women
welcoming me into a coven.
No long line of shape-shifters
welcoming me into a world of magic and power.

Not even my father is here
to study me and take notes
and write papers and books
about his own   daughter—

All I have in this moment,
are the pain, Marisol, a tub
and the truth of what I'm becoming—

It's happening.   It's really happening.

"The thing inside of me, inside of us . . .
does it know things? Does it see things?" I ask.

"Yes. Monsters have souls too.
But those souls have
different rules for living."

"Will there be blood?"
I finally ask. Because I know   I know
that is the last thing I will see before—

"Fireblood," I say.
"Like lava and ash.
We are small volcanoes when we shift."

My answers will not be enough for her.
She has to go through it herself.

In one of her father's books
is a drawing of us
with fangs and claws,
flame and lightning.

I don' know if this is true.
I've never seen my fire self
in the mirror.

Genevieve is in the tub hugging her knees
and hiding her tears, and her skin
is glowing red as the

sun sets and casts its shadow
over the icy white streets.

Everything about this moment is
a kaleidoscope of colors—
And maybe,   maybe
shifting is the most beautifully
human thing,
and I say,
"You will have to fuel your fire.
Who hurt you, Genevieve?"

Do I even have bones?
Do I even have a beating heart anymore?
These are not the questions
I ask, because Marisol and
my mother were right.
    Science can't explain
how I'm glowing like embers
and even my own tears can't
    cool the burning—

And she asks who hurt me.
After a long minute of firebreaths,
I say, "Lourdes. Lourdes hurt me."

                    This is a fancy bathroom and both Genevieve

and I can fit into the tub with enough
room to spare. So I quickly disrobe and
climb in with her, wearing nothing
but my deep brown skin

as it glows like hers—
except she is bright crimson
and I am   maroon.

The house is empty and quiet,
and if anyone comes bursting in
to see us like this,
I cannot stop
what will happen to them.

"How could your own mother hurt you?"
I ask, even though I already know the answer.

"She let my father take me!
I spent my whole life not knowing
who she is—
You had her to yourself all along.
You had her for your entire life
and she's just now coming into mine,"

Genevieve says through
quiet sobs.
I don't want to comfort her
because there is no one to comfort me

as my own skin starts to simmer.
I am used to this, she is not.
I can breathe through this, she will cry.
I can ease out of my skin, she will
have to fight her way out
so she does not   burn herself—

"You had your father," I say.
"My mother took mine from me.
He hurt her. So she swallowed him."

And this is the first time I say this out loud.
This is the first time I name this pain.

So here we are,
two half sisters comparing our lives
as if we ever had a choice between day and night;
war and peace;   lightness and darkness.

"Who hurt *you*, Marisol?"

she asks.

I face her, looking for the truth	I face her, looking for the truth
in my reflection;	in my reflection;
in this nighttime version of me—	in this daytime version of me—

Who hurt me?
A nameless and faceless
mother
who left me with a curse
for a skin;
who left me with nightmares
for memory;
who left me with a scientist
for a father—

Who hurt me?
The boys on the
corner
whose eyes are darts
and I am the target,
my body's a bull's-eye
as their wide, preying hands
grope every part of me so they can
feel the sun—

Who hurt me?
This world is a house of mirrors
reflecting back to me how
pretty I am—
in movies and on TV;
on social media and billboards;
on runways and stages;

Who hurt me?
A name and a face for a
mother
who gifted me a blessing
for a skin
gifted me memory
for nightmares;
who gifted me a ghost
for a father—

Who hurt me?
The boys at the
resorts
whose eyes turn away
and I am a dark shadow,
my body is like smoke
as their wide, preying hands
shoo me away so they can
see the sun—

Who hurt me?
This world is a house of mirrors
reflecting back to me how
ugly I am—
in movies and on TV:
on social media and billboards;
on runways and stages;

I am   everywhere
like the sun
casting a light on all the world
and sometimes
I want to shatter the glass,
burn it all down
just to be able to see what lies
beneath the surface of my own
skin—

I am   nowhere
like darkness
casting a shadow on all the world
and sometimes
I want to shatter the glass,
burn it all down
just to be able to see my beauty
reflected in the glow of my own
skin—

GENMEAVRIIESVEOL

Skin

Lourdes is in the doorway to the bathroom
    dressed in all white as if
she will conjure some old magic
I've only read about in fantasy books—

She has come back for me.
And I am   the daughter of a witch.
But why do I feel so   powerless
right now?

"There are no windows here!"
Lourdes yells at Marisol.
"There are no windows here!"

But Marisol is hugging her knees
and hiding her tears like me,
shaking, in pain too; shifting too.

"There are no windows here!"
Lourdes says again, and tries to pull
me out of the tub, but her hands on
my skin are   like hot iron
and I hiss and pull away—

I already know   I already know
        that there are no windows here—

I already know   I already know
        what happens when the new moon
                is out of sight;
        when the sky is inaccessible.

             But I did not know
           that I would be shifting too.
             I did not know
          how I would make it out
        before Genevieve burned down
this house   that is not
               my home—

And I did not know
        that Mummy would be back so soon
to catch me in this   lie—

        "What are you trying to do?"
        she asks through clenched teeth,
staring at me as she
        grabs Genevieve by her thin arm
        whose skin is becoming liquid—

        I am trying to be free,

I want to say. But instead I tell her,
"We cannot use the mortar.
Where were we supposed to go?"

There are stories of soucouyant
who shift inside closed houses;
who shift behind locked doors
and sealed windows

and that is how they accuse us of
burning down places, homes, and
one time, an entire resort.
We are guilty when
the only thing left standing
is a wooden mortar unscathed
and forged by our own fire.

What else am I supposed to do
when I am trapped in a house
that is not my home,
where my life is not my life?

"The roof, Mari," my mother says.
"You were supposed to take her to the roof.
Don't you see that this will be
the perfect home for us?
We can easily get to the open sky.

So many mortars to choose from.
Or did you want your sister to burn
our home, just like you wanted
me trapped in the night sky?"

Our home?   *Our home?*

"Yes," I tell my mother.
"Just like you want me trapped
in this life, this dream of yours.

I never wanted the sun.
I never wanted the sea.
I never wanted this name.
I never wanted this life."

My own words   my own words
are talking the fire out

and I do not need
my mother in this moment,
but she is here.

She is here,
not for me,   but for her—

All my life, all my seventeen years
of living,   the only thing

I ever wanted;
          the only thing
I was ever hungry for
was   my mother—

And here she is, picking up the Bible
Marisol left on the floor
      and she starts to pray—

What good is God right now?
What good are words I can't even
understand when my insides are
combusting   and igniting
and   this   hurts   more than anything?

My thoughts become a blank page,
a white-hot light of   nothing—

Like this   is the beginning of
everything,   hatching out of some
cosmic egg   or something. *Something.*

So   I open wide   wide
and let out a   scream—

"Genevieve," my mother whispers
like in my nightmares,   except
now the fire   stops burning and it

swallows me,   or I swallow it.

"Her name is Kate. You will know

where to   find her,"

my mother says with the voice I remember

from my   nightmares—

And all I see is a darkness so thick

and then a   light so bright—

And all I feel is a pain so deep,

and then a   hunger so infinite

          that I reach for it

with every cell in my firesoul,

          I reach for it—

I   am   a mermaid

shedding scales and fins—

I   am   the ocean

rising tides, crashing waves—

I   am   the moon

waning and waxing—

I   am   the universe

expanding and contracting—

I'm   meteor   and comet.

I'm   both   witch and monster.

I'm   both   fire and fury—

MGEANREIVIESOVLE

Soul

Genevieve makes a sound
so gruesome, so primal
that I am sure she can be heard
all the way down the block—

I have never seen new soucouyant
writhe their bodies with such ferocity.
It is as if,   it is as if
this thing inside   of her
will try to   kill her
if Mummy is not careful.

There are no windows here.
I need windows—
I will need   to   get out!

"Her name is Kate," I hear
my mother say, but she is not
talking to me, and it is too late,
it is too late to protest,
to reason with Genevieve
and let her know that even
as monsters, we can still do
the right thing—

Kate?

I understand. But she is my mother's enemy
and not Genevieve's.

Mummy's prayers are not for me anymore.
Mummy's prayers do not conjure my flames.
Mummy's prayers are distant and she is
no longer a guiding voice nor a guiding light
charting my way across the sky.

She doesn't give me a name before it is time—

And she pulls Genevieve out of the tub
with the strength of all the soucouyant
who came before her, and carries
her other daughter out of the bathroom
while I am left   alone—

I become a raging ball of fire   and
hunger has pulled me out of my skin,
out of that tub, and I am searching and searching
for an exit—   open sky—
free air—

There are nothing but walls and doors
and—

"This way, this way," I hear my mother say.

Hunger is the thing that pulls me up towards

an opening to the roof and cool, free air,

the night sky and   the new moon—

I fly past Mummy's prayers

that are not for me,

and out of that house

that is not my home;

and past everything

that is trying to

extinguish

all that I am.   *Ugly*

echoes all around me

and I remember the name;

I remember the face;

I remember the soul—

Micah   Micah   Micah   Micah

But in this moment,

he is no longer my enemy—

Kate   Kate   Kate   Kate

is the only thing that propels me

across the sky like a rocket—

Time is   a flash of light.
And shifting,   and flying
is like knowing   how to cry
for the first time.   This is like
knowing how to   open my eyes
to the world for   the first time.
This is like   remembering
how to breathe   and inhale the life
that already   belongs to me—

I didn't know   that when it comes to
monstrous hunger,   I wouldn't question
what I do for   survival—

MARGIENSEVOLIEVE

Monster

"Remember, my daughter.
No good, no evil.
Only consequence,"
our mother's voice echoes
across the sky
as if she is already
up here with us—
"If you focus on the hunger,
you will aim for anyone to satiate it.
But if you focus on the hurt,
you will aim for its source.

Feed the pain so that it can fuel
your rage and launch you
even higher to kiss the sun.
And do not ever
turn to see your reflection
in a mirror."

I seep through everything
like air.

And there she is—
In a hotel room in

I seep through everything
like air.

And there he is—
In a hotel room in

downtown Brooklyn	downtown Brooklyn
together and alone.	together and alone.
Kate Kate Kate Kate	Daniel Daniel Daniel Daniel
is sprawled out on the bed	is sprawled out on the bed
tired from all those nights	weary from keeping the
they stayed up with the twins.	truth from his daughter.
I'm a flash so quick, so swift—	I am a flash so quick, so swift—
She's not just my father's wife,	He is not just my sister's father,
she's food and fuel—	he is food and fuel—
I hover and descend	I hover and descend
and inhale	and inhale
deep like	deep like
I'm swallowing	I'm swallowing
everything	everything
that has ever hurt me—	that has ever hurt me—
And she's not	And he is
Kate Kate Kate Kate.	Daniel Daniel Daniel Daniel.
She's my mother's enemy.	He is my mother's enemy.

I didn't know I didn't know   Mummy told me Mummy told me
that a mirror stood in the far corner   to never look at my monster self
of the room and light reflects   in the mirror and light reflects
back to me everything that I am—   back to me everything that I am—

Smoke and fangs and claws.   Smoke and fangs and claws.
Hunger   and flames—   Hunger   and flames—

I become like a thousand   I become like a thousand
shooting stars   shooting stars
ready to launch across the sky—   ready to launch across the sky—

That was the first time;
That was the first time
I have ever seen myself like this—
Mummy warned me   Mummy warned me
and I wonder
what she is trying to protect us from.
The truth?

Power felt and power witnessed
is an explosive thing   like the BIG BANG

and I am reborn into something
even more powerful
because   because for the first time,
I went after my own vengeance.

No one told me that this monster self

can feel   guilt;

can feel   dread;

can feel   shame—

I'm afraid of what I'll do if the world

ever, ever   threatens my survival—

And I spiral   spinning all over the place

like a tornado— How   How   How

did I become like this?

I'm something   that could only come

from every   hurt and every bad thing

ever done   to all my mothers;

                 to all my sisters.

And—

There is something else in here,

a looming presence that I can feel

behind me, inching closer,

clipping at my firewings—

I ease out as quickly as I came in   I ease out as quickly as I came in

and home is where my mother is, and home is nowhere my mother is,

the keeper of the mortar where   the keeper of the mortar where

I have to   I cannot

return to my skin and become
human again. I did this all for
her—

even return to my skin and become
human again. I did this all for
myself—

MARISGOELNEVIEVE

Shift

Mummy is waiting on the roof with open arms—
Her white dress and head tie are a lighthouse
until   until   I remember the comet
that trails behind me—

She is not as sure of her path in the sky;
she is not as graceful with her flight.

Did she know I was following her?
Did she know that we were
in the same room,
going after the same
family?

Genevieve is new to this,
too fresh to know that on a night
like this, there are always
other beings lurking,
looking for their own prey
and we always have to
watch our backs—

And I descend

and descend

as Mummy watches,
waiting, guiding me
back to
the skin in her mortar—

It was still
supposed to be   *her* mortar.
No one else's skin
was supposed to be in there.

This protector
is handed down
from mother to
daughter through
the generations
of soucouyant,
and
I never knew
my grandmother;
I never knew
the mothers
who came
before her—

And this mortar,
that is storing
the skin that is not

                              my mother's skin;
                          the skin that is not
                                  my skin
                          was supposed to be

                                      mine
                                      mine
                                      mine!

                                  So I aim
                      for the pulsing, glowing
                    mass of beautiful flesh
                    nestled deep within the
            cracks and crevices of this
                      wooden heirloom—

II
Now I know for sure,
I know for sure that
everything in this world,
everything in this universe
has   a   soul—

A soul is
a force that propels us
towards our purpose—

A soul is
an energy that guides us
home wherever we may be
in the cosmos or on this planet

and that is how I see her—

I see her and I've dreamt of this.
I've dreamt of my little girl self
running towards my mother
after falling or getting hurt
or a bad performance and she
embraces me with open arms
and this is where I find   home—

But   but
another flash of light dashes towards her
and lands
and lands
and lands
in the mortar where Lourdes
told me to leave my skin—

And I remember her words;
I remember the last thing
she said to me as I shifted into
this cosmic monster. I was too scared

to listen, I was too much in pain
to understand, but now—

"I named you Genevieve
because you are my first daughter,
and you will represent us in the world.
Woman of our race, woman of our kind.
And this, first daughter, now belongs to you,"
she'd said—

And I fall
and fall
and fall
looking for that soft place to land
but there   she is—
settling into my skin
as if   this is what she wanted all along.

I circle the roof like a bird of prey—
like a flickering light about to go out.

What do I do?   *What do I do?*

III

I land as a shimmer of light,
the skin comes to me

like a moth to a flame.
I am air filling the balloon
that is my
new   skin.

Everything still burns.
Everything is   too tight.
Everything   is like
already worn clothes—
a secondhand,
hand-me-down outfit,
except this skin is older than me.
It should be too big, but instead
I am too big for it,
I make it fit   anyway because

this skin is mine now—

My mother takes this face
in her hands and kisses the skin,
kisses the cheeks over and
over again as if she is praising me
for this new thing I did,
but she doesn't know.
She doesn't know—

"You did good, Genevieve,"
she says, and I want to cry.
"Come. We must guide your sister."

And she takes the hand that is not my hand
and everything is still too tight,
too small for this big life of mine.

Lourdes rushes to the door
leading down to the brownstone
and all I need to do is get back in,
get back into   a skin,
but   a blurred version of me
is holding Lourdes's hand and I can't
make sense of anything right now
because I need skin, flesh, brain, and heart
to make me   human   again—

I bolt through the door and I find hers
there in the tub, glowing and pulsing
with a life that's not my own—

But I need it like I need air
after being underwater for so long.
The skin comes to me like a magnet
and it makes a sound like a vacuum,
like the universe contracting

into this body, this skin
this life   that is not mine.

This is not mine!
I want to yell   but all I can do right now
is catch this human breath and hear this human heart
beating   beating   beating—

This is not   *my skin!*

"You did good, Marisol," I hear Lourdes say.

MARISOLGENEVIEVE

Kin

I didn't know that hunger
was a deep well that could
hold all of humanity—

But only if I want to fill it
with rage. I'm that angry.

Lourdes is busy pouring ice
into the tub and the faucet
is against my back and if
it weren't for the cold water
forcing me to be still and let
everything settle and sink in,
I would lunge at her.

I would devour her
with her own hands—

Instead   instead
I hold on to the edge of the tub
from exhaustion, from weakness

and breathe   breathe like a dragon.

I stare   at myself
I stare   at myself
sitting in the tub directly in front of me,

our legs touching, and I want it back!

I want myself   back.
I can't form the words.
I can't make a sound
other than   firebreaths.

"Marisol," Lourdes says to me.
"Who was it? Who did you go after?"

I'm not Marisol!
I want to shout
but everything is frozen solid
as if this skin has made
me into a chiseled sculpture,
a replica of my half sister.

I don't look away from Marisol
as my mother calls me by her name
and I know she hears it—

I open the mouth that is not my mouth
to speak but—

"Kate?" I ask, and the voice
that is coming out of this body
startles me. It echoes
in my core and it is as if
my soul and this new skin
are just getting to know each other.
"Why did you tell me to go after Kate?"

And my thick accent is gone.

"No."

Genevieve makes a sound I can
barely hear. But I cut her off before
she says anything.
"Why Kate?"

"Oh, Genevieve," Mummy says.
"You do not know that I have been
dreaming of this day since you left.
I have always wanted to show you
the wonder of what you are. I have
always wanted to show you your
power and to be your one and only
mother—"

"No!"
is all I manage to say.

How is it that I can feel so full
and so weak at the same time?

I try to climb out of the tub,
but these legs are not my legs.
This skin is a smooth dark brown
and it's wrinkly from being
in the cold water
for so long
and
I don't want it.

I   don't   want   it!

"What is wrong with you, Mari?
You know you have to wait.
Give yourself time to heal,"
Lourdes says, and she gently
guides me back into the tub.
I pull away from her.

That sudden move makes me
even more tired.

"No," I whisper again,
and it took all my strength to
speak with a voice that's not mine.

Marisol didn't just take my skin,
she straight-up hijacked my soul—

And I can't do anything
except sit here and cry
and stare at someone else
wearing my hair,
        my face,
                my skin.

And she   is smiling
wide   knowing
that she is stealing   my life—

                    "Mummy," I say,
                but I quickly catch myself.
                "Mama. What's happening
            to your skin? Is it your turn?"

                    I can play ignorant.
                    I can play princess.
                I can play the other daughter.
                    I can play dancer.
            I can play   pretty
                              pretty
                              pretty.

I can see myself sitting there in the tub—
my deep brown skin;
my short, tightly coiled afro;
my curves and my soulful eyes—
Genevieve wears my skin
as if it is an old dress
that is out of style.

I wear hers like the ones my soucouyant
sisters and I would go shopping for—
fresh, enticing, and a magnet for the boys.

Genevieve is tired, too tired to fight me
and it will take a couple of days before
she gains back her energy and begins to live
the life   of a true soucouyant;
begins to live life in the   skin

given to me by them—

Black, girl, poor, immigrant.

And I wonder how she will feel
when Micah, her boyfriend, calls her
ugly   ugly   ugly   ugly—

And we are both still   incomprehensible.

Mummy touches the arm that is not my arm.
"Genevieve," she whispers. "You should be the one
who is tired. Not Marisol. She is used to this.
Why do you have so much energy after shifting
and flying? Heh? What is going on?"

"Lourdes," I say with audacity.
"It is your turn now. You have to go
before the sun rises, right? Or else . . ."

It is not my voice saying this.
So it gives me courage
to do what I need to do.

I can always say, Genevieve did it.
And   it will be true—

Mummy breathes and breathes and breathes
and she knows she must go find her mortar.
And tonight, the moon is on my side

letting this mother and her two daughters
shift and fly on the same night—

"It is time for you to go, Lourdes," I say
with Genevieve's voice, and face, and skin.

And Mummy stares and stares and asks,
"Marisol, is that you?"

And I play dumb. "What?"

"How dare you! How dare you commit
such an atrocity!"

But Mummy cannot hold it in any longer.
Her skin is becoming hot coals and for her,
the process is quick, painless, but even
more so ravenous—

I have never asked her,
I have never asked her
who she goes after—

She rushes up to the roof, leaving me
with Genevieve's soul in my skin;
leaving me in Genevieve's skin
in this tub, in this house
that is not my home.

But now,
maybe   maybe
this can finally be home.

Until   until
the next new moon—
"I want it back!"

Genevieve says with my small, tired voice.
I hear my accent—and I wonder
when I would have ever gotten rid of it.

"Until the new moon," I plead.
"Let me borrow it until the new moon."
I can get used to this voice,
to these flat words that make me
sound more American.

Now I am wearing the skin
given to me by them—
Black and white,
girl, middle-class,
American.

And pretty
pretty
pretty.

And I am—Genevieve is
a hurt, bruised, weak, sorry girl
that cannot help herself/myself.

My heart breaks

for myself and her.
She will know what I've been feeling.
I will know what she's been feeling.

This heart that is not my heart
is beating fast, like it's an igniting
thing that can spark a fire inside me.

But it's not the new moon and
I've already shifted, but I need a do-over.
I need to reverse this. I need to go back
to my own skin—

And my mother leaves me here
in her other daughter's skin—
To feel her pain.
To feel my pain.

It's me! Genevieve! I want to yell.
But in this skin, will anyone believe me?
Will anyone know that I'm trapped, trapped, trapped—

"Dad," I whisper, because he will know.
He will know that I am in here, trapped.

"Dad!" I yell with all my strength,
and I almost pass out.

"I am sorry," I whisper
when I hear her call out for her father.
"I am so sorry, my sister."

I get out of the tub, leave the bathroom,
and step into her room
with all her clothes,
with all her makeup,
and begin to prepare

for tonight's
performance.

I try on her clothes.
I put on her makeup.
I smile and laugh
and toss this hair back.
I pull it up into a bun,
I brush it down,
I run my fingers through it.
I twirl in the mirror.

Tonight, I will dance as if my
life depends on it.
It does. It does.

But I want to dance to something
other than Beyoncé's "Pretty Hurts."

Pretty hurts?
How could pretty
bc a painful thing?

MARISOL——GENEVIEVE

Dream

And when the sun rises,
flooding all the windows
in this house with new light, a new day,
this new life settles on me like dust.

Genevieve will soon realize
that her father will not answer
her call for a while.

"What did you do?"

she asks
as she comes down the stairs,
wearing my clothes.
My hair that is her hair now
is flat on one side, and I will
have to teach her how to care for it.

I toss her hair that is now my hair
over my shoulder.
The thick, curly tresses hang
against this skin like a warm coat.
I can get used to this—

I could fight her now.
I have my energy back.

But who will I be hurting
if I give her a black eye,
some scratches on her face,
pull her hair? I'll be hurting me.
"What did you do?" I ask again.

She's standing in front of me
as calm as an ocean breeze,
and she already knows that
if I hurt her, I'll be hurting me.

                                    "Something I'm not supposed to do,"
                                         I say, and I don't know what
                                              the price will be for this.

                                    "Daniel will think he has the flu,
                                              and so will Kate,"
                                                   I tell her.
                                    "Mummy will be able to help
                                              with the babies."

"I missed last night's performance.
I need to dance tonight.
You're going to ruin my life!
Getting into Juilliard School. Micah. *Everything!*
And you don't even have a life for me to ruin.
This is not fair!" I say. "This isn't an even exchange!"

"You can still have those things.
Show me how to dance like you.
But I don't want Micah.
He's been cruel to me and
he hasn't been kind to you either.
How he treats you is not love, Genevieve.
And you can have my mother to yourself."

I'm quiet for a while, thinking about this
bargain; thinking about what she said about
Micah. She doesn't know Micah. She doesn't
know my life. But still, what can I get out of this?
Will this be like borrowing clothes?
Maybe Marisol will wear my skin better.
Maybe I will wear Marisol's skin better.

And slowly, slowly,
I begin to surrender to this defeat.
I look at my/her arms and touch the skin—
how smooth it is, how beautifully brown it is.
I reach up to feel the soft tufts of hair on this head,
and think of all the ways I will style it.
Marisol has no idea how I'll be able to level her up.
She has no idea of all the ways I'll make her look better.

"No wigs, no harsh chemicals," I tell
my sister when I see her touching her/my hair.

I stare at her/myself.
Slowly, I begin to realize it.

There is no better mirror than seeing
your own skin worn over
someone   else's   soul.

The sunset is just as beautiful as the sunrise.

"You are pretty," I say to Genevieve.
To myself—
I step back to get a better look
at her/myself. All the angles
I've never seen before.
I am seeing myself
for the first time
through someone else's eyes—

I touch her hair on my head.
I hold out her hands with its
sunny skin dotted with freckles,
like bits of Mummy were sprinkled
onto her to remind her of who she is.

"The hair needs to be washed every other day.
Don't let it get frizzy," I tell Marisol.

My phone rings nearby. It's Micah.
He's been calling and leaving messages since
last night when I missed the performance.
He can't find out about this.
He can't know that it's me in Marisol's skin.
And   she can't   have him—
I don't answer, and say to Marisol,
"You have to break up with him.
You have more courage than I do
to say it to his face that he's an asshole."

                              "It will be my pleasure,"
                        I say, and she hands me the phone
                        because Micah is video calling her.

                                    I hesitate for a moment
                                    because this means
                              I will have to be an actress too.
                        I answer it, but instead of Micah's face,
                        I see Jaden, smiling, with a hint of
                                    mischief in his eyes—
                              "Jaden? What are you doing
                                    with Micah's phone?"

                        Genevieve tries to come over to see,
                              but I put up a hand to stop her.

"Sweetness," Jaden says.
"This was the only way
I could find you again."

"Don't call me that,"
I say. Even with Genevieve's
face, I am still a
soucouyant. She is a
soucouyant too. And he is
still forbidden—

"No problem. But I wanted to
tell you that your boyfriend
came to the bakery with another girl.
And he . . .
He left his phone here,"
Jaden says, and his jab jab
lies don't work on me.
His tongue is no longer
red, which means . . .

‖
I didn't know that Island Bakery
was a hub for all the Caribbean
spirits to gather in the morning
and buy bread after a night of
feeding on souls—

Now that I'm truly one of them,
my eyes have opened up to all the magic
that's always been here in this part of
Brooklyn. My father can never know.

Marisol and I came here when she told
me what Jaden is. Jab jab. His stories
are in my father's books too. But those
stories don't tell the whole truth. Those
stories are old and those writers, like my
father, don't know that when shape-shifters
move from one place to another, their
magic shifts too. Jab jab are not only
carnival characters who come out at
dawn. Here, they feed on the souls of those
who have harmed them. Or harmed the ones
they   love—

Jaden must've done something to Micah.

                    "Where is Micah?" I ask Jaden when I
                        reach the counter after standing
                            in a long Saturday morning line.

                    I tell Genevieve to wait outside and
                        keep her face hidden. I don't want
                    Jean-Pierre nor his wife to see me/her.

We can't forget the skin we're wearing.

"Coconut bake? Or coco bread?"
is all Jaden says, smiling. Then he
slams a phone on the counter.

"He wasn't nice to you,"
Jaden says as he bags our bread.
"And he wasn't nice to my friend
over there either." He glances at
Genevieve in my skin. She came into the
bakery even though I told her not to.
And Jaden smiles even brighter.
He winks at her/me
in that smooth way that island
boys do when they're flirting.

The customers behind us force us
off the line before I can even make
sense of what just happened.
"He likes you?" I ask Marisol.

She just nods.

"We need to find Micah.
We need to know if he's okay."

"He will be," I say,
not sure if it is true or not.
I don't know what kind of
monster Jaden is.

Before we walk out of the bakery,
he calls my name. I turn around.
Genevieve doesn't.
We both forgot again who we're
supposed to be—

Jaden comes from around the counter
and whispers to me,
"You came here to dream, eh?
Well, I see that your dreams have
come true.   Marisol."

And he knows. He knows—

"I get off from work at three.
Come see me," he says to me
in Genevieve's skin—

We need to go find Micah.
We need to see if my father is okay.
We need to get the twins.
We need to find our mother.

Why, in this moment,
do I feel like I'm losing everything
and everyone? And Marisol
is over there using my skin
to flirt with that boy?

That black cat leaps from behind
the counter and rushes to me
so fast, my heart plummets.
It sits there in front of me,
looking up and meowing like
I'm its mommy or something.

"Let's go, Marisol!" I call out,
annoyed. Then I remember.
Shit. Shit. Shit.
"I mean, Genevieve."

Jaden takes one look at
me and holds a finger up
to his lips. "Shhh," he says.

The cat wraps its furry body around
Genevieve's leg/my leg and
she tries to shoo it away
but it's persistent in claiming
her as its owner—

"I guess your boyfriend
has found you. Cats have a way
of recognizing souls," Jaden says
to Genevieve in my skin
and he takes the next customer.

Genevieve and I stare at him—
Mouths open, eyes wide.

And I can't believe, I can't believe
what Jaden has done.

"Micah?" I whisper, staring at the cat.

I've heard of these stories.
How jab jab can snatch
a soul and fling it into
someone else's body—
human or otherwise.
A temporary vengeance
that only lasts a full moon cycle,
thank goodness.
The victim learns their lesson
to never mess around
with a jab jab;
to never mess around
with monsters
who rule the night—

I let a long minute pass and
wait for most of the customers
to leave before I go back to Jaden
and whisper with a wicked smile,
"What have you done, Jab Jab?"

He winks at me.
I know   I know.
We do no ask and we do not tell.

Then Jaden says,
"What do you think of the name
Carnival Bakery? It was always
my dream to own a business
in America—
Living is dreaming too, you know.

And I don't like that skin on you.
I can't wait for you to give it back.

I just smile back and say,
"I'll see you next new moon, then."

I've done everything that is forbidden,
so why not this? Why not kiss a jab jab boy
to see what magic it will ignite?
And I do not ask if he really wants
me or my sister.

And I do not ask how Jean-Pierre
and his wife are doing, either.
The place is buzzing with workers, and
the owners are nowhere to be found.

I was supposed to be allergic to cats.
Kate loves cats, and she rehoused
the one we had when my skin
condition started. But now—

I pick up this bakery cat.
And this shit is wild!
I look into his eyes.
I see.   I see him.
And I wonder if Micah knows that
whatever he did, he fucked up.
He fucked up big time—

And he sees me too.
He sees me past Marisol's skin.
"I don't think it's gonna work out,"
I say to the cat; I say to Micah.

III

We have another night to ourselves
in this house that is now my home.
It's true. Kate and the collector
are sick like dogs—

Body aches, headaches, coughs . . .
The flu, maybe.

Soucouyant, definitely.

The twins are safe with Kate's sister.
And Mummy. Where is Mummy?

How is this my life?
I'm now a dark-skinned girl
with a Caribbean accent
and I'm a fur mom to a cat who
is housing my ex-boyfriend's soul.

I broke up with Micah.
It was easier to do it through a cat.
"You're a fucking asshole, you know that?"
I'd said after he followed me and Marisol home.

And he just meowed. And maybe it was
his way of saying that he still loves me
and thinks that I'm still beautiful.
Even while in Marisol's skin. I hope.
"That's what you get
for being such an asshole!"
I tell the cat/Micah.
"And picking a fight with a carnival monster!"

And where is our mother?

"I wanted her to see me dance,"
I say to Marisol after I missed another
night of the performance.
"I wanted her to finally
be   my mother."

                              "She's coming back," I say,
                    even though I know   I know
                         we broke something in the
                                     order of things—
                         We stand there in her father's
                              living room with all the art,
                                 with all the storybooks
                                    about girls like us—

                         I want to try to fix what we broke.
                         So I hold my right pinky up
                              and say to my sister,
                         "Let me try this on for a while.
                         I'm just borrowing it until next time.
                              I promise to give it back."

"Whether you give it back or not,
I'm taking it back," I say,
and hold my finger up too.

"What? You don't want to live life
in my skin? You don't want to
walk and fly through the world as
a true   soucouyant?"

I know what she means.
But I tell her the truth.
"I want what's mine. I want
the true version of my story.
And you should too. Isn't the truth
more beautiful than the myth?"

"No," I say to my sister.
"The myth is more beautiful
than reality. I still want to dream.
How come I am seen as more
monstrous than you? Let me be
seen as human for awhile."

I want to tell my sister that it shouldn't
matter how she's seen. But even I know
that's a myth too.   The kind of myth
that is   a lie.

So we lock our pinkies,
making a promise to each other

that we will be sisters in flame,
sisters in magic,
and what is hers is mine,
what is mine is hers—
until each new moon.

Together, we go up to the roof
to search for our mother.
We wait and wait and wait
until dawn and—

She should've been
back already because
the sun, the sun
casts a light
into our mother's mortar—

still with her skin, still with her skin
as it withers and dries
in the sun's muted heat—

And we look up at the sky and wonder
how deep is this crack in the universe
that we have caused—

How deep is this crack in the universe that we have caused?
She should've been back already.

She should've been back in her skin,
back to her human self,
back to her mother self.

So I squeeze my sister's hand
knowing what this big magic,
this secret exchange
has cost us;   has cost her.

"I'm sorry, Mummy," I whisper
to the hidden cosmos, to the hidden stars
behind the morning sun
because this is the life she wanted
for me, anyway—

To dream.

"Where is she?"

Genevieve asks
with her/my voice shaking.

"Home, maybe," I tell her.
"She finally went home."

I pull my sister close
and this is the first time
I see myself crying,
shedding real tears for a mother

whose secrets were as vast as
humanity itself.

"I wish I could have your memories too,"
I say to Marisol as I cry on her shoulder.
My shoulder. "I wish I could remember
what it was like to be   a daughter."

                    "You are still her daughter, Genevieve.
                          When you look in the mirror
            and you see my face—
            deep brown like the earth,
                          nose and lips like our ancestors,
            black like the night,
                          and with magic as old as the universe,

            you will know that you are
                    the daughter of all the mothers before you—

            And you can still be   my sister."

So I take her hand in mine.
Our skins are
light and dark, sunrise and sunset,
day and night—sisters   under the same
sun,   moon,   and stars.

Author's Note

Welcome to the magical, expansive, and, at times, creepy world of Caribbean folklore! I'm thrilled to be sharing my contemporary fantasy debut based on the story of a skin-shedding witch who turns into a fireball at night to find her victims and sip from their life force. Sometimes it's their blood, sometimes it's a bit of their soul. This witch is known by different names throughout the Caribbean: soucouyant in Trinidad, lougarou in Haiti, and old hag or hag in Jamaica and Barbados. These are all variations and combinations of vampire and witch lore—old women who often live alone in the forest who need to feed on others (sometimes babies!) to sustain their own lives.

These stories often depict the older women as having gruesome features and serve as a metaphor for the cycle of life—birth, death, and the afterlife. But in (S)Kin, one teen girl is also the soucouyant or lougarou, and she needs the life force of others to sustain her own magic, while the other girl is questioning whether or not she has inherited any shape-shifting magic at all. If you believe in folklore like I do, these wonderful beings walk among us, hiding in plain sight.

I was born in the Caribbean, where stories like these are relegated to the past or the deep forests and the rural parts of the islands. But like all people who want a better life, magical beings can have dreams too. There is so much more out there than hunting victims who have wronged you. The possibilities are endless when you have the power to shift out of your skin. Trade in the beautiful Caribbean landscapes with its sunshine and blue sea for the urban landscapes of high-rises and bustling streets and the rules of magic will change—for better or worse, depending on who is wielding that magic. So begins the story of a teen soucouyant immigrant trying to find her way in a world that already sees her as a monster, and another teen girl coming to terms with what's been hidden from her and what lies dormant beneath her own skin.

I've decided to write this story as a contemporary fantasy novel in verse because poetry and lyricism are an important part of Caribbean storytelling. Not all magic can be explained, but its truth is hidden in the unseen and unspoken parts of a story. And in poetry, the line breaks, the white space, the wordplay, the word placement, and the metaphors all tell another story, the real story. Magic and reality are like siblings, like kin. And sometimes, magic doesn't change what's real, and what's real doesn't change what's magical. With *(S)Kin*, I ask you, the reader, would you risk your own magic, your own power, for a taste of someone else's?

Happy reading!
Ibi Zoboi

Acknowledgments

I first wrote this story as my graduate thesis for my MFA program. It wasn't a novel in verse then, and it highlighted my clumsy attempts at writing speculative fiction featuring my own culture. I'm so glad I have the opportunity to return to my love of speculative fiction and pair it with my love of poetry. Thank you so much to Alessandra Balzer, who saw the possibility in this story and helped shape the very seeds.

I'm so grateful for Weslie Turner who guided me toward the finish line. Your insight and cautionary editorial eye allowed me to see the bigger story, the magic as metaphor. Thank you to Luana Horry and my team at Versify/HarperCollins.

Huge thanks to Elena Giovinazzo for being an anchor.

To my daughters, who always bring a fresh and youthful perspective: 'preciate you.

Shout out to my team at Balzer + Bray/HarperCollins: Patty Rosati, John Sellers, Audrey Diestelkamp, Shannon Cox, Mimi Rankin, and Caitlin Johnson.

A special thanks to illustrator Salena Barnes for portraying Marisol and Genevieve so beautifully. As always, to Jenna Stempel-Lobell for bringing that special touch to the design.

I'm grateful to my first readers. Amber McBride, thank you for your generous words. I am a Day One fan!